"It's standard procedure for me to interview people before I hire them, Grace," Jack said.

She straightened her shoulders and lifted her chin. "By asking them who they've slept with? I'm sorry, but that's getting a bit personal for me." Her gaze deliberately swept up and down his body. "Maybe you should remember the old saying about those without sin throwing the first stone, because I doubt you've been living like a monk."

Her words angered him, but the hot blaze in her green eyes excited him like nothing he could remember. He wanted to jerk her into his arms, smother her lips with his. It was crazy! She was a stranger, and a pregnant one at that....

Yet the feeling was there. And it felt glorious to a man who'd been emotionally dead for a long, long time.

Dear Reader,

Looking for sensational summer reads? All year we've been celebrating Silhouette's 20th Anniversary with special titles, and this month's selections are just the warm, romantic tales you've been seeking!

Bestselling author Stella Bagwell continues the newest Romance promotion, AN OLDER MAN. *Falling for Grace* hadn't been his intention, particularly when his younger, *pregnant* neighbor was carrying his nephew's baby! Judy Christenberry's THE CIRCLE K SISTERS miniseries comes back to Romance this month, when sister Melissa enlists the temporary services of *The Borrowed Groom*. Moyra Tarling's *Denim & Diamond* pairs a rough-hewn single dad with the expectant woman he'd once desired beyond reason…but let get away.

Valerie Parv unveils her romantic royalty series THE CARRAMER CROWN. When a woman literally washes ashore at the feet of the prince, she becomes companion to *The Monarch's Son*…but will she ever become the monarch's wife? Julianna Morris's BRIDAL FEVER! persists when *Jodie's Mail-Order Man* discovers his heart's desire: the *brother* of her mail-order groom! And Martha Shields's *Lassoed!* is the perfect Opposites Attract story this summer. The sparks between a rough-and-tumble rodeo champ and the refined beauty sent to photograph him jump off every page!

In future months, look for STORKVILLE, USA, our newest continuity series. And don't miss the charming miniseries THE CHANDLERS REQUEST… from *New York Times* bestselling author Kasey Michaels.

Happy reading!

Mary-Theresa Hussey

Mary-Theresa Hussey
Senior Editor

Please address questions and book requests to:
Silhouette Reader Service
U.S.: 3010 Walden Ave., P.O. Box 1325, Buffalo, NY 14269
Canadian: P.O. Box 609, Fort Erie, Ont. L2A 5X3

Falling
for Grace

STELLA BAGWELL

Silhouette
ROMANCE™
Published by Silhouette Books
America's Publisher of Contemporary Romance

To my musician buddies,
The Lutie Outlaws.
Thanks for letting me sit in.

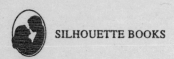 SILHOUETTE BOOKS

ISBN 0-373-19456-0

FALLING FOR GRACE

Copyright © 2000 by Stella Bagwell

Visit Silhouette at www.eHarlequin.com

Printed in U.S.A.

Books by Stella Bagwell

Silhouette Romance

Golden Glory #469
Moonlight Bandit #485
A Mist on the Mountain #510
Madeline's Song #543
The Outsider #560
The New Kid in Town #587
Cactus Rose #621
Hillbilly Heart #634
Teach Me #657
The White Night #674
No Horsing Around #699
That Southern Touch #723
Gentle as a Lamb #748
A Practical Man #789
Precious Pretender #812
Done to Perfection #836
Rodeo Rider #878
*Their First Thanksgiving #903
*The Best Christmas Ever #909
*New Year's Baby #915
Hero in Disguise #954
Corporate Cowgirl #991
Daniel's Daddy #1020
A Cowboy for Christmas #1052
Daddy Lessons #1085
Wanted: Wife #1140
†The Sheriff's Son #1218
†The Rancher's Bride #1224
†The Tycoon's Tots #1228
†The Rancher's Blessed Event #1296
†The Ranger and the Widow Woman #1314
†The Cowboy and the Debutante #1334
†Millionaire on Her Doorstep #1368
The Bridal Bargain #1414
Falling for Grace #1456

Silhouette Special Edition

Found: One Runaway Bride #1049
†Penny Parker's Pregnant! #1258

Silhouette Books

A Bouquet of Babies
†"Baby on Her Doorstep"

*Heartland Holidays
†Twins on the Doorstep

STELLA BAGWELL

sold her first book to Silhouette in November 1985. Now, nearly forty novels later, she is still thrilled to see her books in print and can't imagine having any other job than that of writing about two people falling in love.

She lives in a small town in southeastern Oklahoma with her husband of nearly thirty years. She has one son.

IT'S OUR 20th ANNIVERSARY!
We'll be celebrating all year,
Continuing with these fabulous titles,
On sale in July 2000.

Intimate Moments

 #1015 Egan Cassidy's Kid
Beverly Barton

 #1016 Mission: Irresistible
Sharon Sala

 #1017 The Once and Future Father
Marie Ferrarella

 #1018 Imminent Danger
Carla Cassidy

 #1019 The Detective's Undoing
Jill Shalvis

#1020 Who's Been Sleeping in Her Bed?
Pamela Dalton

Special Edition

 #1333 The Pint-Sized Secret
Sherryl Woods

 #1334 Man of Passion
Lindsay McKenna

 #1335 Whose Baby Is This?
Patricia Thayer

#1336 Married to a Stranger
Allison Leigh

#1337 Doctor and the Debutante
Pat Warren

#1338 Maternal Instincts
Beth Henderson

Desire

 #1303 Bachelor Doctor
Barbara Boswell

 #1304 Midnight Fantasy
Ann Major

#1305 Wife for Hire
Amy J. Fetzer

 #1306 Ride a Wild Heart
Peggy Moreland

#1307 Blood Brothers
Anne McAllister & Lucy Gordon

#1308 Cowboy for Keeps
Kristi Gold

Romance

 #1456 Falling for Grace
Stella Bagwell

 #1457 The Borrowed Groom
Judy Christenberry

#1458 Denim & Diamond
Moyra Tarling

 #1459 The Monarch's Son
Valerie Parv

 #1460 Jodie's Mail-Order Man
Julianna Morris

#1461 Lassoed!
Martha Shields

Chapter One

He was back! Her prayers had been answered!

Heedless of the late hour, Grace Holliday whirled away from the living room window and hurriedly searched the floor for her sandals.

Since they were nowhere in sight, she quickly decided she didn't need shoes and flew out the door to scurry across the dark lawn toward the bungalow next door. Part of the structure was hidden by pines and magnolia trees, but she hadn't dreamed the light shining in the kitchen. She could see it plainly now.

The yellow shafts filtering through the pine boughs were like a beacon to her weary heart and in spite of her growing girth, she felt as light as air as she skimmed up the wooden steps and across the planked porch.

The solid wooden door was open to the ocean breeze, and through the screen she could see the small living room was dark. No sound stirred from within the house, making her wonder if he'd fallen asleep.

Rapping her knuckles on the jamb, she called out, "Trent! Trent, it's me, Grace. Are you in there?"

Seconds dragged into a minute as she stood in the muggy darkness, anxiously awaiting his answer.

To her left, parked beneath the small carport next to the porch was a late-model sedan of an indistinguishable dark color. It wasn't the vehicle Trent drove while he'd stayed here in the bungalow, but he could have easily changed cars since she'd last seen him.

"Trent! Answer the door!"

Another long minute passed without any sort of response and she decided to enter the house and make herself known to him. Surely he hadn't heard her knock. He wouldn't just ignore her. After all, he'd come back to Biloxi. That had to mean something.

Inside the shadow-filled living room, she called again, "Trent! Where are you?"

Moving toward the light in the kitchen, she entered a short hallway. Suddenly the floor creaked behind her, and then a male voice lifted the hair on the back of her neck.

"Who the hell are you?"

Her heart hammering, she whirled around, then unconsciously inched backward toward the light and away from the dark bulky image of a man looming in front of her.

"I—I'm Grace Holliday. Who—are you?"

"Obviously not who you were looking for."

His deep voice was full of sarcasm and just a hint of warning. Unwittingly she moved several more steps behind her, until she was completely illuminated by the dim overhead light in the kitchen.

"I thought—I was looking for Trent," she said haltingly.

"I know. I heard."

Her brows lifted with skepticism. If he'd heard, why hadn't he answered her knock? she wondered. Slightly irked, she asked, "Is Trent here?"

The man suddenly moved into the light and it was all Grace could do to keep her hand from flying to her mouth as he stopped within inches of her.

"Why do you want to know?"

"I...thought—he—"

Her disconnected words halted completely as her gaze tried to access everything about him at once. Aside from being tall, he was lean and fierce-looking with hooded gray eyes, a square set jaw and chiseled lips, which at the moment were pressed together in a grim line. Hair the color of a lion's mane curled ever so slightly against his collar and fell in a thick wave straight back from a broad forehead. Grace realized she was looking at one irritated but very sexy man.

"You thought he...what, Miss Holliday?"

Nervously she licked her lips, then pulled her gaze away from him to glance around the room. Funny how nothing in the cozy little kitchen had changed since Trent had come and gone. She supposed the only thing his presence had changed was her.

"Nothing. I...saw the light from next door and thought it was him. Sorry about the mistake."

The young woman standing in front of him had a messy blob of coal-black curls piled atop her head. She was wearing white shorts and a loose red T-shirt. Her feet were bare and the legs connected to them were long and firm and shapely. But her legs were not what riveted his attention. It was the rounded protrusion evident beneath the swell of her breasts that quickly caught his eye. The woman was pregnant! Very pregnant!

The discovery distracted him, making him momentarily lose his train of thought. Which was a cardinal sin for a man in his field of work.

"My name is Jack Barrett," he finally said.

She extended her hand to him and Jack felt inclined to take it rather than rebuff this pretty intruder. Which wasn't like him, either. Jack didn't usually give a damn whom he snubbed. Beautiful women included.

"Are you—did you buy this place, or something?" she asked in a faintly bewildered tone.

As he clasped her soft hand in his, he decided she couldn't be more than twenty-two or three. Jack quickly racked his brain, trying to remember if Trent had ever mentioned a girl named Grace, but that was like fishing in a lake for a minnow. In the span of a work week he heard more names than most people heard in a year. And it wasn't as though he associated with his nephew on a regular basis. Since his sister's boy had grown up, Jack rarely saw the young man.

"Or something," he said as he suddenly decided to move cautiously with Grace Holliday. If she'd been involved with Trent, there was no telling what she might want. But with the Barrett family, it usually boiled down to one thing. Money.

"Tell me, Miss Holliday, do you usually enter other people's houses at night like this?"

A blush stole over her cheeks and Jack noticed that even though her face was bare of makeup, it was still rich with color. Delicate black brows and thick lashes, pale green eyes and skin that was tanned to a deep rose-brown. The image of a Tahitian goddess, he decided. Sensual, earthy, and naturally beautiful. Just the kind that ruined a man's common sense.

"No," she answered. "But the door was open and I thought—"

One corner of his mouth lifted in a sneering sort of smile. "And you thought Trent was here."

She nodded and he could see disappointment all over her face. What did it mean? he wondered.

"Do you live here in Biloxi?" he asked.

She nodded again. "In the house next door. That's how I met Trent. He was staying here earlier this year."

Jack racked his brain again. Trent had finished college at midterm break back in December. He tried to remember if he'd told Trent he could use the beachside bungalow after that time. Not that it would have mattered if his nephew had used the house without his consent. Jack had never seen the place until today.

Two years ago he'd bought the piece of real estate on a whim. An employee with the firm had needed quick cash and Jack had written him a check without much thought to what he'd do with a beach house in Mississippi.

Two years was a hell of a long time to finally get curious about a place.

The words his secretary had spoken to him yesterday suddenly popped into Jack's mind, putting an even deeper twist on his lips. He'd started to tell Irene that nothing could rouse his curiosity anymore. He'd done and seen too much. But he was glad he hadn't. Because Grace Holliday would have made him out to be liar. She was doing more than rousing his interest.

"Uh...how long has it been since you've seen this— Trent?"

She grimaced as she considered whether to tell this man anything. "I—look, I don't know you. Maybe I should just apologize for the intrusion and be on my way.''

Folding his arms across his chest, he eyed her suspiciously. ''You've already said you were sorry once. That's enough. But if you weren't a pregnant woman, I would think you'd walked in here to steal something.''

Her green eyes widened with disbelief, then filled with insult. ''I'm sure because I *am* a pregnant woman you're thinking all sorts of things anyway.''

He was. But not the sort of things she believed he was thinking. And suddenly Jack decided he couldn't let her know he was Trent's uncle. At least, not for now. If he expected to find out who she really was and if her baby had any connection to his nephew, he was going to have to be very guarded about himself.

His gaze dropped to her left hand. There was no engagement ring or wedding band of any sort and she hadn't corrected him when he'd addressed her as Miss.

''You're not married to this Trent guy?''

She shook her head as a puzzled frown creased her face. ''Why would you want to know?''

He shrugged one shoulder. ''No reason, actually. But the way you were calling his name—you sounded pretty desperate to see him.''

Grace had been desperate to see Trent. Five months had passed since he'd left her and the baby behind. And during that time she'd mostly accepted the fact that he didn't want her in his life. Especially on a long-term basis. But she'd hoped—prayed—that he would return for the baby's sake.

''Yes,'' she quietly admitted.

When she didn't elaborate he asked, ''Are you...planning on marrying this guy?''

A sad little smile curved her full lips. The expression bothered Jack more than he cared to acknowledge.

"No."

His brows lifted ever so slightly. "Is he...the father of your baby?"

A shadow crossed over her face, closing it off to Jack.

"I'm sorry," she said again. "But I—have to get home now. Goodbye, Jack Barrett."

For a moment, as she stepped past him, he considered latching onto her arm and stopping her. But he didn't. She obviously didn't want to talk to him. And he was in no position to press her without making himself appear suspicious.

When he heard the screen door softly bang behind her, Jack walked to the front of the bungalow and peered through the front screen.

Grace Holliday was crossing the small lawn in the direction of the house next door. Her head was down, her steps slow. No doubt she dreaded going home to face her parents with the news that it hadn't been Trent she'd found next door, but an older, wiser and much more hardened man.

Hell, he very much doubted Trent was the father of her child anyway. If his nephew had stayed in the bungalow earlier this year, he'd no doubt brought friends along with him. If there was one thing Jack did know, Trent had always had plenty of buddies hanging around him. She could have gotten tangled up with one of Trent's friends and was now looking for him to help her in some way.

One way or the other, Jack was going to find out. If for no other reason than his sister's sake. Jillian was ten years older than Jack and had been divorced almost as many years as Trent had been living. The boy's father had skipped out not long after the kid had been born, leaving Jillian to raise her son alone. The last thing his sister needed was for some money-hungry young woman to slap a lawsuit on her son.

By the time Grace entered the house and sank onto the side of the old four-poster, she was visibly trembling.

Clamping her hands together, she closed her eyes and willed the image of Jack Barrett away. She didn't know who he was or why he was in Trent's house. Yet one thing had been clearly certain, he hadn't taken kindly to her little visit.

Tears stung her eyes, but she blinked hard, determined to keep them at bay. It was far too late for tears or disappointment, she fiercely told herself.

Still, when she'd first seen the light in the bungalow her heart had soared. She'd been certain Trent had come back. Not for her. No, any hope she'd had for the two of them had died months ago when she'd first told him about the baby. The news had forced him into admitting he'd never really loved her. And had never intended to have a lifelong relationship with her. He'd simply come to Biloxi for a bit of fun and to wind down from final exams at Texas University in Austin.

After the initial shock and pain of being used had worn off, Grace had accepted the fact that she'd been a fool. And slowly the feelings she'd had for Trent had died. But since then she'd kept hoping, praying, he would return for the baby's sake. She wanted her child to have a father. She wanted her son or daughter to know it was loved by both parents. And tonight, for a brief moment as she'd raced to the bungalow, she'd thought her hopes had come true.

Instead she'd discovered a man quite unlike any she'd ever encountered. Sensuality had oozed from every pore of his body. Just looking at him had made her quiver with an awareness she'd never before felt.

She'd not allowed herself the time to ask if he'd had a family or if he were planning to stay for a while. Getting away from his prying gray eyes had been of the utmost urgency in Grace's mind. Yet even now, in the safety of her bedroom, she could still feel his gaze on her face and body.

He was not the sort of neighbor she would have chosen to have move in beside her. A big family with lots of happy, rowdy kids would have been more to her liking than Jack Barrett. From the look on his brooding face, she'd gotten the impression he'd wanted to either clamp his fingers around her neck or kiss her.

Shivering at the thought, she reached over and switched off the lamp at the head of the bed, then slowly undressed in the darkness. She had to forget about the man. Tomorrow was going to be another long, tiring day. She had to be rested and ready.

The next morning Jack's secretary, Irene, answered his call on the fourth ring.

"What in hell are you doing?" he barked into the receiver. "Eating bonbons?"

"No, trying to seduce one of your clients. But he hightailed it out of here after the third ring. You have rotten timing, Jack. Besides, what are you doing calling the office? The doctor wanted you out of this place for a while, remember?"

Heaving a weary sigh, Jack tilted his head back far enough so that he could get a view of the house next door. Early this morning, before he'd cooked himself breakfast, he'd watched Grace carry an armload of books and a straw tote bag out to the car parked in the driveway. Her black hair had been down on her shoulders and the sea wind had whipped strands of it across her face and tugged at the tail of her long flowered skirt as she'd lowered herself into the little compact car.

Moments later she'd driven off in the direction of Gulfport, and so far she hadn't returned. Nor had anyone else stirred around the big old house.

"I'm not in the office, Irene. I'm merely talking to you."

"I don't know why. You said you didn't give a damn if you ever saw this place again," Irene reminded him. "You said you never wanted to hear another phone, alarm clock, radio or TV. And you especially didn't want to hear a judge's rulings, a witness's testimony or a client whining for a larger settlement."

"That's true," he said curtly. "And I meant every word."

He set his empty coffee cup on a low table in front of the couch, while Irene made a sound that was somewhere between a laugh and a sigh.

"So you're quitting Barrett, Winslow and Layton?"

Was he? Jack asked himself. In his eyes, quitting was akin to losing. And Jack had never lost a case in the courtroom. He didn't know how to lose. But the job was getting more and more meaningless. And so stressful that two days ago he'd wound up in his doctor's office with a stomach full of fire and blood pressure high enough to kill him.

For thirty minutes he'd listened to the doctor lecture him about burying himself in his work and not taking time out for life outside his law practice. Hell, Jack didn't have a life outside the office and he'd told the doctor so.

"Then you'd better get yourself one before you wake up with no life at all," he'd told Jack.

"You haven't answered, Jack. Are you quitting the firm?" Irene repeated her question.

"That would make Dad especially proud," he said mockingly.

"John Barrett is dead, Jack," she said bluntly. "There's no reason for you to keep trying to please the man now."

John Barrett. For years just the mention of the name had been enough to make corporations shake in their boots. No business large or small wanted to face the formidable lawyer in the courtroom.

From the time Jack had been a small boy he'd been groomed to follow in his father's footsteps. Generations of Barretts before him had built the firm of Barrett, Winslow and Layton. Jack was expected to keep it going. Nothing else would have been acceptable in the eyes of his father.

"I didn't call to get into a psychological discussion with you this morning, Irene. I need a little information and I was wondering if you'd seen or talked to Jillian lately."

After a pause Irene said, "I don't remember exactly when I last spoke with your sister. A couple of weeks ago, I think. She stopped by the office to see you. But you were in court that day."

"What did she want to see me about?"

"Hmm. Nothing special that I recall. I think she just happened to be out shopping and dropped by on a whim. Why?"

"Did she mention Trent?"

"I asked her about him," Irene explained. "She said he was doing fine. Especially now that he'd started at his new job."

"What about a girlfriend? Did she mention one of those?"

Irene laughed. "Well, Trent has gone through a list of girlfriends. Sort of like his uncle, you know."

Letting his secretary's snide comment slide, he said, "I'm talking about a special one."

"Trent thinks each one is special. Until he gets tired of them."

"I didn't ask for your opinion on my nephew's behavior, Irene. Just the facts."

That he was treating the conversation as lawyer to a witness didn't bother Irene. After fifteen years of being his secretary she was used to his brusque, plain-spoken manner.

"Sorry, I got carried away for a moment. Must have been all that sugar from the bonbons," she replied. "But as for a name, I do recall Jillian mentioning some girl he'd been seeing steadily. I believe it was something like Tessa or Tricia."

Not a Grace. Jack didn't know how he felt about this bit of news.

"You're sure?"

"Not a hundred percent. But I do remember it was a *T* name. Does that help?"

"A little."

"Now, are you going to tell me what this is all about?"

"No."

"Oh, well, why should that surprise me," she said with mock hurt. "I'm just the old faithful secretary that puts in sixty hours a week for you. I don't deserve an explanation."

He rolled his eyes. "Irene, if I thought I could do without you, I'd fire you."

He could hear a wide smile in her voice as she replied, "But you can't do without me, Jack. So you won't fire me. Besides, I'm the only real friend you have."

She was so close to the truth it made him wince. The fact that his fifty-five-year-old secretary was his very best friend said a damn lot about his life.

"There's nothing to tell," he said crossly.

"Well, frankly, I don't understand, Jack. I thought you went to Biloxi to get away from the stress of this place, not investigate your nephew."

"I'm not doing an investigation, Irene," he said tiredly.

There was a long pause, then she asked, "So how long are you planning to stay down there?"

"I don't know. It all depends."

"On what?"

His beautiful pregnant neighbor, Jack thought.

Out loud he said, "My mood, Irene."

"Hmm. Well, I hope you're in a better one the next time you call."

"So do I," he rumbled, then hung up the phone before she could say more.

Rising from the couch, he walked out onto the porch and gazed at the Gulf of Mexico. A brisk south wind was white-capping the water and pushing the waves onto the beach. The stretch of empty sand was no more than seventy-five to a hundred yards away and ran parallel to the front of the house. At the moment egrets and gulls screeched and swooped over the rolling salt water, some strutting boldly upon the white sand in search of a scrap to eat.

He couldn't remember the last time he'd been in Biloxi. He thought it might have been seven years ago. Vaguely, he recalled a case he'd been handling at the time. A casino had been suing a building contractor for some reason that escaped him now.

Since then, several more casinos had sprouted up along the beaches of the coastal resort town. But surprisingly, the added traffic and noise was far removed from this place, which, being some three miles away from town, had somehow managed to stay quietly sheltered. Other than the house next to him, there were no other residences around.

Jack couldn't imagine Trent staying in such a quiet, isolated place. He always remembered the boy liking bright lights and excitement. Jack figured a plush room in one of the casinos would have been more to his liking. But then, he had to admit Grace Holliday would be an attraction in her own right for any young man. Perhaps between her and the gaming tables, his nephew had kept himself entertained and content with the place.

Damn it, what was he doing? He was already making the supposition that Grace Holliday was carrying Trent's child. And that could be the furthermost thing from the truth.

If Jack were being completely honest with himself, the simple fact that Grace was carrying a child, no matter who had fathered it, bothered him. Though he didn't understand why. Nowadays unwed mothers were the norm rather the exception. Besides, she was a total stranger to him. How she chose to live her life was none of his business.

Yet last night, when she'd offered him her hand, he'd

sensed something different about her. It was almost as though she were a Southern-bred lady with pride and morals and family values. Not some woman who would sleep with a man, then try to extort money from him.

Hellfire, Jack, he silently cursed himself. You've been in the courtroom too long. You can't see a gold digger when one is standing right in front of you.

Hours later, a squeaking noise grew louder, intruding on the fringes of Jack's slumber. Damn birds, why didn't they go back to the beach where they belonged? he wondered drowsily.

Another screeching squawk pierced his ears and popped his eyes wide open. Above his head, he saw a network of pine boughs swishing in the gentle breeze. Where the hell was he?

Scraping his fingers through his hair, he sat up on the chaise longue and through squinted eyes glanced around the small backyard. Everything came back to him with sudden clarity. The doctor's grim edict. The long drive from Houston to Biloxi yesterday. The weariness he'd felt last night before Grace Holliday had made her uninvited appearance in the bungalow.

The memory of his pretty neighbor had him quickly glancing at the place next door. She could be home now. He hadn't been watching; he'd spent most of the afternoon working on brief for a major upcoming trial. He'd come outside for a break and the last thing he remembered was sitting on the longue, listening to the lulling sound of the restless ocean and drinking in the scent of pine and salt water.

He must have been more tired than he'd thought to have fallen asleep like that. His lips twisted ruefully at the thought. Another clue that he was getting old and burned out.

Rising from the longue, he started for the house, then stopped dead in his tracks as Grace's voice floated over to him.

"Joshua, don't let your instrument sag. What have I been telling you for the past three weeks? You must keep it up and level at all times. Now, hold it there and start again. And this time don't disappoint me."

Jack's eyes opened wider. The woman wasn't in any condition for kinky, afternoon sex, was she?

Not less than fifteen feet away, a chain-link fence, along with several head-high azalea bushes, separated the two backyards.

Not knowing what to expect, he walked to the fence and peered through the bushes. About ten feet away, on a brick patio, Grace was standing with her back to him. Her hair was once more piled atop her head in a mass of loose curls. She was still wearing the yellow blouse and long skirt he'd seen her in early this morning.

As for the reprimanded Joshua, there was no sight of him. Then suddenly the squeaking noise that had awoken Jack moments earlier began again. Grace stepped to one side, giving him a bird's-eye view of the culprit.

He appeared to be about eight years old. A shock of brown bangs threatened to jab his eyes and his tongue stuck from one corner of his mouth as he concentrated for all he was worth on the small violin tucked beneath his chin.

A music student! God help him, he'd come here for peace and quiet. This was the most torturous noise he'd ever heard in his life! And Grace Holliday couldn't be a music teacher. She was too young. Too pregnant!

Women like her didn't do things like this, he silently argued.

"That's much better, Joshua." She spoke again. "But you're letting your bow slide. Remember you must keep it straight with the bridge. And level."

"Yes, I remember, Miss Holliday. But when I'm thinking about the notes my fingers have to make, I forget about the bow," the youngster complained.

Jack watched her give the boy an encouraging pat on the shoulder. "I know you do, Joshua. But soon it will all come together for you and you'll be playing Strauss in no time. I promise."

Strauss! Hell's bells, this kid couldn't even play the scales. Was she loony?

Jack didn't wait around to hear more. The screeching sounds of horse hair pulling and pushing against metal strings filled the backyard again, drowning out the breeze and the call of the seagulls.

He escaped into the bungalow, glad he had the windows shut and the air conditioner running. It was time for dinner, anyway, he thought. He'd fix himself something to eat, then maybe later, after "poor little Joshua" was gone, he'd find some way to talk to Grace again.

This time he intended to get some answers.

Chapter Two

Two hours later, the screeching and sawing was still going on. At the moment the offender was a redhead she called Albert. He'd come in after a towheaded boy who couldn't have been more than six years old had pulverized Jack's eardrums as he'd attempted to grill pork chops outside.

By now Jack was beyond trying to think up some legitimate excuse to talk to the woman again. Hours of this agonizing noise had given him ample reason for another confrontation.

Grace was unaware anyone was around until she felt a tap on her shoulder. She whirled and her mouth formed a perfect *O* at the sight of his tall frame towering over her.

"Uh…what are you doing over here?" she asked bluntly.

Jack asked himself the same question. He was a stranger around here. An interloper. Someone who would only be here for a short time, whereas this was her home. He didn't have a right to complain or question her.

Unless she was planning something detrimental to his nephew, he quickly reminded himself. And there was no way of knowing that without acquainting himself with the woman. But that didn't mean he had to be nice about it. Which was a good thing, because at the moment Jack was feeling anything but nice.

His jaw tight, he asked, "What do you think I'm doing?"

Her brows disappeared beneath a fringe of black bangs. "I wouldn't know," she answered curtly.

Disbelief widened his gray eyes, then his lips twisted into a mocking line. "I'm sure you never once imagined you've been dealing me some misery."

Quickly she glanced at Albert, who was still struggling with the G-scale. Then casting her gaze back on her unexpected visitor, she asked, "I beg your pardon?"

He snorted at her innocent response. "Do you realize the noise you're making over here?"

The man needed kicking in the shins. But with Albert present, she did her best to curb the unladylike urge.

"Would you mind stepping over here?" she asked, gesturing to a grouping of redwood lawn furniture positioned several feet away from Albert. "I don't want my student distracted."

Before he could reply, she'd turned and left him standing with his hands in his pockets.

"Look, Miss Holliday," he said after he'd followed her to the secluded area where several chairs and a table were shaded by an enormous live oak. "I didn't come over here to sit and have a chat with you. All I want is for you—"

Jack's words halted as his eyes fell past the full thrust

of her breasts and on to the large rounded bulge of her midsection. He'd not been around many pregnant women in his life and the ones he had, he'd not found attractive. But this one—there was just something about her that left him feeling wet behind the ears.

"For me to do what, Mr. Barrett?" she prompted.

He heaved out a disgusted breath. Then biting back the words he really wanted to say, he said, "Last night I didn't tell you, but I plan to be here for the next few days."

He hadn't really told her anything about himself last night, Grace thought. But then, she hadn't exactly stuck around to ask him. She'd found the man more than disturbing and this evening the feeling hadn't lessened— in fact, it had intensified.

She couldn't be certain about his age, but he appeared to be somewhere around thirty-eight or forty. That prime age when a man just can't look any better. And this man was definitely at his peak, Grace decided.

He had the lean, muscled body of an athlete. His rough-hewn features, coupled with his thick mane of hair and cool gray eyes made him one of the most striking men she'd ever seen in her life.

"Really? So you've bought the bungalow from Trent?"

It wasn't like the boy to lie, Jack thought. At least, he didn't think so. But then he had to remind himself the Trent he remembered being around had been a teenager. Maybe he'd changed since then. Or maybe this woman was subtly trying to draw information from Jack.

"The place belongs to me now," he said evasively.

Once again he could see a shadow of disappointment cloud her green eyes.

"I see," she said quietly. "So that means..."

"Means what?" he urged.

She shook her head, then forced a wan smile to her face. "Nothing."

For the first time in his life Jack was at a loss for words, making him glad his associates weren't around to see him. He'd tackled hundreds of hostile witnesses, wrangled words with some of the most formidable judges in the country and never lost his ability to lead the conversation to where *he* wanted it to go.

But with this woman, words failed him. All he could do was stare and think. And feel things he shouldn't be feeling. What in the hell was the matter with him, anyway?

"Look, Miss Holliday, I came to Biloxi for some peace and quiet. I didn't expect to find this." He jerked his head backward toward Albert and his screeching instrument.

His clipped statement appeared to take her aback and for a moment Jack thought he saw a wounded look in her eyes, as though it pained her that he was being unfriendly. But, hell, that was a crazy notion. She didn't even know him. It couldn't matter to her whether he was Mr. Nice or a real jerk.

She folded her arms beneath her breasts. The movement made the mound of baby she was carrying even more evident to his gaze. "Surely Trent told you about me."

His eyes narrowed. "What about you?" he asked carefully.

She frowned as though she considered his question inane. "That I was a music teacher, of course. And that you might encounter...well that some of the music might spill over onto your place from time to time."

The idea that she called these boys' squawking efforts "music" made him want to laugh out loud. But at the same time he'd been expecting her to come out with something much more personal about Trent. The fact that she hadn't, disappointed Jack greatly. He was anxious to get to the truth. And even more eager to get away from this woman. She bothered him in ways he couldn't begin to understand.

"Actually, he didn't tell me anything. I...purchased the property through a Realtor," he lied. "Yesterday was my first day to ever step foot on the place."

Her expression said only a fool would buy a piece of property without looking at it first. And it dawned on him that she didn't have any idea he had money to burn. The amount he'd paid for this little spot on the beach had been insignificant to him.

"Why?"

Jack frowned. "What do you mean, why?"

"Why did you buy this place without looking it over first?"

Impatient with her question and even more with himself because he found her so damned intriguing, he asked sharply, "Do you think that really concerns you?"

She took a seat on the edge of one of the chairs and crossed her sandaled feet. Jack's gaze was instantly drawn to her toenails, which were painted a rich, lusty red. How the hell she managed to reach them, he didn't know. But then, maybe she had a man who'd been glad to paint them for her. The idea grated on him far worse than the sound of Albert's resined bow.

"No. It really doesn't concern me at all, Mr. Barrett. Just as my music students don't concern you."

Slowly he folded his arms against his chest. "I'm

sorry, but that's where you're wrong. And as for calling that—'' he gestured back over his shoulder toward Albert ''—'music', I think you need to have your ears tested.''

She cast him a too sweet smile. "If you're bothered by the music, perhaps you should go inside.''

The grin he shot back at her was anything but sincere. "Why don't you go inside?'' he suggested.

Straightening her shoulders, she stared him in the eye. This man was way too arrogant for his own good, she decided. "For one, my air conditioner is not working. It's hot inside. Two, I want to get the children accustomed to playing out of doors. Since they'll be putting on an outdoor concert this fall for one of the local elementary schools.''

He snorted with mocking disbelief. "Concert! For the past two hours I haven't heard one decent note from these kids!''

Her lips compressed to a flat line, she rose to her feet. "Will you kindly lower your voice? I don't want Albert to hear you.''

"Well, I've been hearing him for the past thirty minutes. How much longer is this going to go on?''

Grace took in a long breath and let it out slowly as she tried to compose herself. Of course, anyone who wasn't used to being around beginning music students, especially violin students, weren't prepared for the noise, but this man didn't have to be so rude and insensitive about it all.

"What do you do for a living, Mr. Barrett?''

"I'm a lawyer. What has that got to do with anything?''

It figured, Grace thought. He seemed awfully good

at asking personal questions. "Did you go into the courtroom without training?"

He glowered and she quickly answered for him.

"Don't bother telling me. We both know you had years of it. And even then you weren't an expert. You had to learn. Just like Albert and the rest of my students. And if you do happen to stick around until this fall, I'll show you what I mean."

He'd angered her, Jack realized. Her breasts were heaving up and down in short spurts. The color along her angled cheekbones had deepened to the shade of rich wine. Sparks lit her green eyes and the odd thought struck Jack that he wished he were as alive as this woman standing in front of him. He couldn't remember the last time he'd felt as much passion as he saw on her face.

"I'm sure I won't be here this fall, Miss Holliday. Like I told you earlier, I'm only staying…a few days."

She studied him keenly, making Jack wonder what she saw when she looked at him. An old man? A pesky neighbor? Or was she looking at him in a more personal way?

Hell, Jack, since when did you ever care how a woman looked at you.

Not since his wife, and she'd divorced him years ago.

"What about your family? Are they not staying here with you, too?" she asked.

"No. I don't have a family."

"Oh." The news left Grace feeling strangely warm and disturbed. At his age she'd expected him to have a family. If not with him, then tucked safely away somewhere. Now that she knew he didn't have a wife or children, she felt even more threatened by his powerful presence. "I'm sorry," she added.

He stopped short of releasing a mocking laugh. "Sorry? Look, this is the way I want to be. Free. Single. I'm as happy as a hog in a watermelon patch."

From the looks of him, he'd never been that happy in his life, Grace thought. But then, the haggard lines on his face could be mostly from fatigue. Or anger at her for disturbing his peace and quiet.

"Miss Holliday, it's seven-thirty. My mom is going to be waiting out front."

Giving herself a mental shake, Grace glanced away from the man to see Albert climbing down from the step-chair where he'd been practicing his violin.

"Excuse me," she said to Jack. "I'll be back in a few minutes."

Jack started to tell her it was time for him to go, too. But he stopped himself short. He'd wanted an opportunity to talk to her. Now that she'd given him one, it would be foolish to pass it up.

Jack listened while she gave Albert instructions on what to practice through the coming week. Eventually the boy's sheet music and instrument were packed away and with a gentle smile, she led him by the hand out of the backyard.

As Jack watched, he had to admit, albeit reluctantly, that she seemed good with children. Though he'd never had any kids himself, he could easily remember back to when he'd been Albert's age. Francine, his mother, had been loud and high strung with hardly any time for her son or daughter. She'd never smiled or touched him with the tenderness Grace has just shown Albert. She'd liked her cocktails and the social life that went with being the wife of a highly successful corporate lawyer. She'd seen that Jack and Jillian had the material things

they'd needed, but had never given either of them any
emotional nurturing.

Francine, having divorced their father shortly before
he'd died of a heart attack, had quickly married a
wealthy financier on the west coast. Jillian still shed
tears when she recalled how their mother had treated
them through the years. As for Jack, he didn't give a
damn if he ever saw the woman again.

Pushing the dark thought aside, Jack hitched up his
trousers and took a seat on one of the lawn chairs to
wait for Grace's return.

Five minutes passed with no sign of Grace. Jack was
getting more than a little restless, wishing he'd held his
temper and tongue. He knew from long experience that
badgering a person who held information he wanted
was not the way to go about business. Honey always
caught more flies than vinegar. Trouble was, Jack had
almost forgotten how to sweeten his words and still
manage to sound sincere. He'd used to be damned good
at it, but then, he'd used to want to be a lawyer, too.

"Sorry I was gone so long. But Albert's mother likes
to talk."

He glanced up to see Grace walking toward him.
Quickly he rose to his feet. "Look, Miss Holliday, this
whole thing with your students…let's just forget it. If
you'll be kind enough to let me know when they'll be
around, I'll try to be gone. That way neither of us will
be bothered."

She searched his face, trying to decide if his olive
branch was real. She must have decided he'd passed the
test, because after a moment she smiled.

Her teeth were very white against her creamy skin
and red lips. A faint dimple dented one of her cheeks
and for the first time he noticed there was a tiny freckle

just above the top line of her lip. She was perfectly beautiful. If Trent had been involved with her, Jack could certainly see why. Attraction was stirring deep in his gut, making him wonder if he'd gone suddenly crazy. She was pregnant and a good fifteen years or more his junior!

"Please, call me Grace," she invited. "You're not one of my violin pupils."

Clearing his throat, he said, "All right, Grace."

That he'd conceded to call her by her first name seemed to please her. Her green eyes softened and her lips continued to tilt upward in a provocative smile. "Would you like something to drink. Iced tea? Coffee?"

At the moment he could have used a good shot of Kentucky bourbon, but she didn't look to be the drinking sort. Actually, if it wasn't for her pregnant condition, she'd be the perfect sheltered Southern miss.

"It's hot inside the house," she went on before he could answer. "But I could bring the drinks out here."

She sounded almost eager for his company, making the skeptical part of him wonder why. No doubt she had plenty of male friends her own age. Obviously she'd had one in particular.

"There's no need for you to bother," he told her. "I just had supper not long ago."

"Oh, it's no bother," she assured him. "You wait here and I'll be right back."

Once again Jack took a seat in the lawn chair and as he waited for her to return with the drinks, he made a slow survey of the backyard.

Along with the deep shade offered by the trees, a vine-covered arbor sheltered the brick patio. Potted plants grew in abundance everywhere, lending splashes of bright color to the modest surroundings. From the looks of the house, it needed attention in several places. The paint was particularly weathered and faded from the incessant onslaught of salty sea breeze.

The neglected condition of the house made him wonder what her parents did for a living and why they hadn't made an effort to do better. But Jack wasn't going to be too quick to pass judgment on the people. For all he knew, Grace's parents might be working their butts off to put several more children through high school or college.

Inside the house, Grace momentarily leaned against the kitchen cabinet counter and pressed a paper towel moistened with cold water against her forehead. She was so sick of being hot and tired. So weary of trying to keep putting one foot in front of the other when every inch of her body was screaming to rest.

She didn't know why in the world she'd invited Jack Barrett to stay for a drink. It wasn't as if he was a good friend or even a fond acquaintance. But he was her next-door neighbor. And long before he'd died, her grandfather had passed on his Southern upbringing to Grace. Elias would've considered it downright rude to not be neighborly and hospitable. Even to a stranger, who wasn't so friendly himself, she thought grimly.

But she wasn't going to be too quick to judge Jack Barrett, she promised herself. He might be dealing with a lot of personal problems at the moment. His curt attitude might be hiding a broken heart. He certainly had the look of a man who didn't have much love in his life. And Grace definitely knew how dark and lonely that could make a person feel.

* * *

Only a very short time passed before she reappeared carrying a tray with a tall pitcher and two tumblers filled with crushed ice. As she placed the tray on a small table between them and began to pour the tea, Jack felt a pang of uneasiness, even guilt.

He couldn't believe she was offering him traditional Southern hospitality after the way he'd talked about her music pupils. But then, she could easily have an ulterior motive for being nice to him, just as he had for wanting to talk to her.

"You shouldn't have gone to this much trouble. Not for me," he said, wondering why the hell his conscious had suddenly decided to show its face after all these years.

She handed him one of the glasses, then gestured to the tray. "There's sugar and lemon, if you like. As for the trouble, I have a motive for keeping you here with a drink."

Jack's hand paused in midair as he reached for a lemon wedge. "Oh," he said guardedly. "What is it?"

"Well, I hope you won't be offended, but—"

This brought his head up and his gaze connected with hers. A sheepish little smile was on her lips and he feared he was about to learn the true side of Grace Holliday.

"But what?" he pressed.

She shrugged, then let out a sigh. "I guess I might as well not be bashful about it," she said. "Especially now that I have you here."

His brows lifted with curiosity, but otherwise he remained quiet. Inside his chest, his heart beat with sluggish dread as he waited for her to continue.

Eventually she spoke. "After you said what you did

a while ago about not having family and being here alone, I thought maybe...well, that I might do a little work for you while you're here."

Her suggestion jerked him straight up in the chair. Work! Was she crazy?

"Look, Grace, I don't know what sort of work you have in mind, but I came down here to Biloxi to get out of the office. I only brought one lengthy brief with me and I can manage to type up my own notes."

She tilted her head back and laughed. Jack was too busy taking in the smooth slender line of her neck and the musical sound slipping past her lips to be insulted by her response.

"I don't mean legal work! Good Lord, I don't know a thing about the law. I was talking about cleaning your house. Or maybe doing your cooking or laundry. Any chore of that sort which you might not want to tend to yourself."

House-cleaning, cooking and laundry, in her condition? It was obscene, as far as Jack was concerned. His feelings must have shown on his face because as she continued to look at him, disappointment fell over her soft features.

"Grace, you obviously have a job with your music pupils. Surely your parents don't want you taking on more. Especially in your shape."

Her brows pulled together as a look of total confusion filled her face. "'My parents'?" she repeated blankly. "Jack, I don't have any parents. I live here alone."

Chapter Three

"Alone? You live here—alone?"

The incredulous tone of his voice put a wan smile on Grace's face. "Yes. I do. I teach violin on Tuesday and Friday evenings. The rest of the week, I go to college. So I need all the work I can get."

"But you...you're—" He couldn't say the word and he knew some of his old law cronies would howl with laughter if they could see him now. Stuttering as though he were as green as grass. Damn it, what was wrong with him? There wasn't much he hadn't seen or confronted in his lifetime. Nothing embarrassed him. Nothing really touched him. He was too hard-shell, too used up to let anything get to him.

"Pregnant," she finished for him. "But that doesn't make me an invalid. It only makes me need the money more."

That she wanted money had been in Jack's mind all along, he'd just never expected her to want to work for it. Even now, he still wasn't sure he'd heard her right.

"Aren't your parents helping support you?" he was prompted to ask.

A guarded expression stole over her face as she quickly glanced away from him. "I don't have any parents," she said flatly. "Not in the normal way you're thinking."

"Are they dead?"

His blunt question didn't seem to bother her and it made him wonder if deep down, beneath the smiles and gentle words she'd shown her music pupils, she was just as hard as he was. Jack had learned a long time ago that the female gender was expert at deception.

"My father died from a hunting accident when I was very small. As for my mother—she isn't around."

"Because she doesn't approve of your pregnancy?"

Her brows lifted at his question and then a pained little smile curled the corners of her lips. "She doesn't know about my pregnancy."

"Why not?" Jack persisted.

She frowned at him as he tilted the glass to his lips. "Do you always ask personal questions of strangers?"

Jack supposed he had been coming on a bit strong. He told himself it was because of Trent and Jillian that he was so eager to learn about Grace Holliday's life. Yet somewhere in the deeper part of him, he had to admit he simply wanted to know her, the woman.

"Sorry. It's the lawyer in me, I suppose. Asking questions is akin to breathing to me." Without looking at her, he swirled the amber liquid in his glass, making the ice tinkle against the sides. "I guess the question was a bit nosy."

Grace didn't know what was the matter with her. Normally she never minded personal questions. Even ones that had to do with her flighty mother. But Trent's desertion had changed her. She no longer trusted men. She took every word, every look, very cautiously. And something about Jack Barrett put her on guard even more.

"Why my mother doesn't know about my pregnancy is a long story. One I'm sure you'd find boring," she found herself saying.

He lifted his gaze to her and quickly discovered she was looking at him. The feel of her somber green eyes gliding over his face jerked at something buried between his chest and his gut.

"Maybe. Maybe not," he murmured.

She inhaled a deep breath, then glanced away from him as she let it out. "I can't believe you thought I was living with my parents." She turned her gaze back on him. "I'm twenty-three years old."

She said it as if that was a great old age, as if she had plenty of wisdom to get along in this world alone. Any other time Jack would have snorted at her attitude, but something in her eyes stopped him. Behind her brave stare, there were dark, sad shadows that normally would have taken years to acquire.

He shrugged. "Because you're single, I just assumed you still lived at home with your family. An honest mistake, don't you think?"

She grimaced. "I suppose so."

"Well, since I've already offended you I might as well go on and ask you how you manage to get by on your own like this. Is the baby's father...helping you financially?"

She looked away from him. Jack couldn't help but watch as she pressed the ice-cold glass against her throat and down the open collar of her blouse where it veed just above the valley between her breasts.

"No."

As he digested the one word, he could only think that her baby couldn't belong to Trent. Jillian hadn't raised the boy to shirk his responsibilities.

"Doesn't that make you angry?"

"Humph," she softly snorted. "I don't expect money from him. Having a man's child isn't about money."

He watched her face keenly as he sipped from his glass. "Have you asked him for financial help?"

Her face suddenly turned stony. "No. And I don't intend to. He—Trent doesn't want me or the baby. And I don't want handouts from him—or anyone else."

Trent doesn't want me or the baby. The volunteered information was so unexpected Jack was knocked sideways for a moment. Then doubt swiftly washed in behind the wave of surprise. Even if she did name Trent as the father of her baby, he wasn't going to be so quick to believe her. She might have been involved with a number of young men, but Trent just happened to be the one with money.

"So this...er, Trent you were calling out for last night is the—father?"

Jack took the faint jerk of her head to be a nod.

Frowning he said, "Maybe the guy doesn't have enough money to care for himself, much less a wife and baby," he suggested.

She placed her glass on the table between them, then wearily rubbed her hands against the small of her back. "Trent has plenty of money," she told him. "He spent more in the casinos than I make teaching violin all year."

Jack didn't doubt that. He could see she lived meagerly compared to the standards he and his nephew were accustomed to.

"Is that what drew you to him? His money?"

She scowled at him as she continued to push at her back. The movement thrust her breast forward and, although Jack told himself not to look, he couldn't pull his eyes away from her lush, womanly body.

"What's the matter with you, anyway?" she asked. "Do you have a fixation for money or something? You sure do mention it a lot."

Her suggestion pulled him up short. Jack had never considered himself as having an obsession for money. He'd been born into wealth and as a grown man he'd acquired an even heftier sum of his own. It was something he'd never had to do without. Nor ever would. But Grace was right. He'd mentioned money several times to her in the past few minutes. Did he place too much importance on the stuff?

"No," he answered out loud. "But I—I was just wondering what you'd seen in this guy in the first place. He sounds like a jerk to me. Are you...sure he's the father of your baby?"

She stared at him and Jack knew he'd gone too far as he watched her jaw drop and hot color fill her cheeks.

"I've never met anyone so insulting in my life!" Rising to her feet, she picked up the tray. "Don't bother to bring your glass to the door when you've finished. I'll get it later."

She turned and headed toward the house. Before Jack had time to consider his actions, he jumped from the chair and caught up to her on the shaded patio.

As she reached to open the door he caught her by the shoulder. "I'm sorry, Grace. I was out of line."

The touch of his hand, more than his words, brought

her head around and she glanced pointedly down at his long fingers.

"You're not sorry. You were just being yourself. But that doesn't mean I have to sit around and take it. I'm not one of your witnesses. Now, if you'll excuse me, I have a lot of work to do."

He released his fingers as though she'd scorched him, then jammed both his hands into the pockets of his khaki trousers. "You're mad at me," he said, stunned that it should matter to him.

"No. Disappointed is more like it."

Minute by minute this woman was turning out to be anything than what he'd first imagined her to be, and he didn't know what to think or do next.

"I really wasn't trying to be insulting, Grace. A man looks at these things more logically than a woman. And I was just thinking that maybe you'd be better off if the baby belonged to someone else. Because it appears you're not getting any help from this Trent."

Down through the years he'd sometimes been forced to use a bit of deceit to pull a player into his corner or to swing a case his way. It was just part of the job. But not being totally honest with Grace was beginning to trouble him in a way he wasn't liking at all.

Jack could actually see Irene rolling her eyes in mock disbelief if he were to tell her his conscience had finally made a reappearance after all these years.

Grace sighed deeply, then shook her head. "Look Jack, I've only just now met you. How I manage to support myself is really none of your business. And as for my baby's father, he's out of the picture and I expect him to stay out."

She'd said enough, he told himself. This was all he really needed to know. He ought to thank her for the drink, apologize again, then tell her a final goodbye. Yet, he couldn't let the whole thing simply drop now.

There was still too much he wanted to know before the lawyer in him would be completely satisfied.

"If you'll remember, Grace, you're the one who brought this whole thing up. You're the one who asked me for a job."

Her lips compressed into a flat line. "Yes. And I'm sorry I did. I didn't know you were going to take it as a go-ahead to interrogate me."

Sarcasm twisted his features. "I normally interview people before they come to work for me. It's the standard procedure."

She straightened her shoulders and lifted her chin. "By asking them who and how many they've slept with? I'm sorry, but that's just getting a might bit personal for me." Her gaze swept him up and down in a deliberately leering manner. "Maybe you should remember the old saying about those without sin throwing the first stone, because I very much doubt you've been living like a monk."

Even though her words angered him, the hot blaze in her green eyes excited him as nothing he could ever remember. He wanted to jerk her into his arms, smother her lips with his. It was crazy. She was a stranger—and a pregnant one at that! Yet the feeling was there, anyway. And it felt glorious to a man who'd been emotionally dead for a long, long time.

"I wasn't accusing you of anything, Grace. Just trying to...offer some advice from a different perspective."

She glanced away from him and, though her profile remained rock-hard, he didn't miss her painful swallow or the telltale blink of her long black lashes.

Suddenly Jack wondered if he could be wrong about this woman. Maybe she hadn't purposely set out to snare a rich husband. Maybe she'd been led on, then left to suffer the consequences on her own. Damn it, he couldn't—or wouldn't—know unless he managed to get closer to her. And something told him that might be a very dangerous thing to do.

"I don't need your so-called advice," she said tightly.

"What about that job? Do you still need it?"

Slowly her head turned and her expression was incredulous as she met his gaze. "Are you serious?"

No, more like insane, Jack thought. But he'd already gone too far, he couldn't turn back now. Moreover, he realized he didn't want to.

"Yes. I could use a housekeeper. I wouldn't have much work," he warned. "But maybe enough to help you out."

She appeared to suddenly wilt as a long breath rushed out of her. Wiping a hand across her damp brow, she said, "I'm sorry. I have to—sit down."

She handed him the tray and crossed the few feet to where a couple of wicker chairs were shaded by a curtain of moonflower vine.

As she sank wearily into the chair, Jack moved toward her, his face wrinkled with concern. "Are you ill or something?" he asked.

She shook her head, then, leaning down, began to unbuckle her sandals. "No. Just very tired."

Once the leather straps were loose around her ankles, she looked up to see him still standing inches away, holding the tray she'd given him. "Oh, I forgot. Just put that thing down anywhere. I'll take it in later."

"Maybe you should go in the house and lie down,"

he suggested. She did look exhausted; he wondered if their slightly heated exchange had drained her. He didn't want to think so. The last thing Jack wanted to do was to inadvertently harm her or her unborn child.

Her fingers continued to rub her ankles where the leather straps had fastened the sandals to her feet. "I will later," she assured him. "After you tell me about the job."

Jack placed the tray on a storage shelf by the back door, then took a seat in the wicker chair next to her. "There's not much to tell."

She looked at him, then, smiling wanly, she shook her head. "You and I really have a hard time communicating. I wonder why that is? I thought lawyers were expert at getting to the point."

He couldn't help but smile at that. "Quite the opposite, Grace. We're professionals at drawing people's thoughts off the real issue."

Her brows peaked with sudden interest. "Is that what you're trying to do with me?" she asked warily.

In a way that was exactly what he was doing, he thought a bit guiltily. But this time he had an even better reason than simply looking out for a client's interest. Grace had already admitted Trent was the father of the baby. If true, that meant the child was connected to his family. He had a right to find out where her intentions were headed.

"I'm not trying to do anything to you, Grace," he said, frustration roughing his voice. "Except offer you a little work if you want it."

"I do."

"Good. I don't do house-cleaning. And I know very little about cooking."

Grace couldn't imagine preparing a meal for this

man. Although she'd never had money in her life, she could always spot a person with plenty. And with Jack it was easy to see he was an affluent man by the cut of his hair, the casual, but classic clothes, the Italian leather loafers on his feet, the thin, expensive watch on his wrist.

No doubt Jack Barrett was accustomed to having the best cuisine money could buy. Not to mention anything else his heart desired. Yet as she'd already noticed, he appeared to be anything but happy. The notion made her suddenly remember something her grandfather had often told her.

People with big money are no different than you and me, Gracie. They have their problems, too. Only theirs are bigger.

She said, "I'd better warn you that some of my classes keep me late in the evenings. But on the days I teach violin I'm home earlier."

"Don't worry about it. I'm not on a rigid working schedule."

"Fine. Just let me know when you want me to start."

Jack felt like a fool. He didn't need a housekeeper or a cook. Though he never tended to those chores in his home back in Houston, he was adept at fending for himself whenever need be.

"You haven't asked about the pay," he pointed out.

She kicked off her sandals, then bent forward to place them to one side of the chair. A lock of glossy black hair fell loose from the messy blob of curls and tumbled over one eye. She slowly pushed it back as she looked up at him.

"I trust you to be a fair man."

It had been along time since Jack had done anything to make himself proud. And tonight as he looked into

Grace's weary but provocative face, he wondered to what depths he was going to let himself sink.

"I'm sure we can come to an agreement. Right now I'd better be getting back over to the bungalow. I have work waiting on me." He stepped off the patio, then glanced back at her as he started to leave. "I'll let you know when I want you."

She nodded. "Thank you, Jack."

Another strange twinge of conscious sliced through him, but he did his best to squash it down. He had a lot to learn about Grace Holliday. He couldn't let himself get soft about her now. Or ever.

"Don't thank me yet, Grace. You might be sorry you took the job."

As Grace watched him walk away, she wondered if he just might be right. She couldn't put her finger on just why she found the man dangerous. But something told her he was far more risky to be around than Trent could ever be.

Which didn't make sense. Trent had pretended to love her and then left her pregnant and alone. How could any man hurt her more than that?

As if to answer, the baby kicked hard at the lower part of her stomach. She placed a hand over the spot and felt a measure of comfort. It didn't matter that she had no one else in the world right now. In a few more weeks the baby would come. The two of them would be a family. And Jack Barrett would be nothing more than a memory.

The next afternoon, on his little front porch, Jack glared at the lawnmower that, for no apparent reason, had stalled halfway through the job. He'd checked the gas and oil and found nothing wrong there. The next thing would be to pull the spark plug or tear into the carburetor.

Neither choice appealed to him, but Jack wasn't one to leave anything unfinished. Even something as mundane as cutting the grass. And he sure wasn't going to haul the damn thing into a repairman. Not if he thought he could fix it himself.

Pushing himself off the step, he yanked on the starter rope. After three pulls he muttered a curse and decided there was nothing left to do but fetch his toolbox from the trunk of his car.

As he removed the spark plug from the lawnmower, he couldn't help thinking that he'd come to Biloxi to get away from the pressures of his job. But so far he hadn't felt a bit of relief. Oh, his stomach wasn't burning and the top of his head didn't feel as if it were going to blow off. But he couldn't seem to slow his mind down. It was still going at the rapid speed he worked at back in Houston.

Jack, you ought to be a satisfied man. Irene had said those very words to him more than once. And she was probably right. He owned one of the most successful law firms in the country. His name was synonymous with winning, and he had more money than he knew what to do with. He'd never lacked for female company. Women sought him out. Not the other way around. But where females were concerned, Jack realized money and success were powerful magnets. He'd never been quite sure if any of the women he'd known had wanted him just for himself. Including his wife.

A mocking smile twisted his lips as he studied the blackened gap on the end of the spark plug. Maybe

Irene was right, he told himself. He had all the things most men envied. He should be happy. But he couldn't remember the last time he'd felt contented or at peace with himself.

Rising from his low position, he dropped the plug into the pocket on his T-shirt. The plug was fouled, making the lawnmower useless until he replaced it with a new one. Before he could finish mowing the lawn, he'd have to drive into Biloxi to a parts store.

Heading back out to his vehicle, Jack noticed once again that Grace still wasn't home. Between the work he'd done on the legal brief this morning and the mowing this afternoon, he'd tried not to look over at her place. Or even think about the woman. But last night after he'd discovered she was living alone, he'd not been able to get her out of his thoughts for more than a few minutes at a time.

With a groan of self-disgust, he slid beneath the wheel and quickly twisted the key in the ignition. As he backed out of the driveway, a quick glance to the west told him the sun was sinking fast. After he finished the lawn, a run on the beach before dark might do him good. He needed to sweat and hurt and forget that seeing Grace again was the first thing he'd really wanted to do in a long, long time.

Darkness was creeping in by the time Grace pulled up the short driveway to her house. She hadn't meant to stay out so late, but the class assignment she'd been working on required an enormous amount of research and she'd stayed at the campus library much longer than planned.

On the way back home she'd stopped at the market and bought fresh fish to grill. It was a luxury she couldn't afford, but she'd not had a special meal all week and she was craving anything that didn't come out of a can. Maybe now that Jack had offered her a little work, she would have more money to budget for groceries.

Ignoring her books for the time being, Grace opened the trunk and lifted out the meager sack of food items.

Behind her a male voice said, "Here, let me take that for you."

She recognized his voice instantly and her heart made a funny little leap as she turned around to face him.

"Hello, Jack."

"Hello."

With the back of his forearm, he wiped the sweat from his brow and reached to take the sack from her. "Is this all you have to carry in?"

"My books," she told him. "But they can wait."

"No. I'll get them, too," he insisted.

She fetched the books from the back seat of the car and piled them into his waiting arm. As she did, she tried not to notice the bare muscular legs exposed by his gray gym shorts or the way the navy blue T-shirt molded to the thick muscles of his chest. He'd obviously been running or working out at something. Sweat dampened his longish hair and created a dark triangle on the front of his shirt.

"This really isn't necessary," she told him. "I can manage."

"It's no bother. I was just running on the beach when I saw you pull up."

She started toward the house and he walked beside her. He could smell the faint scent of her perfume, something warm and exotic.

"In this heat, I think I'd rather be in the water than jogging," she said.

"I need the exercise," he said, then glanced at her. "Do you swim? On this beach?"

"When I have the time."

She looked tired. Especially her eyes. And Jack wondered again what she'd been doing all day. He couldn't believe how desperately he wanted to ask her. And not because of Trent or the baby, but simply because he wanted to know.

As they approached the front entrance to the old wood-frame house, she looked at him and smiled. "Did you have a nice, quiet day?"

What would she think, he wondered, if he told her she'd messed up his ability to concentrate on his work? That he would have gladly listened to the awful sound of her violin students, just to have a chance to look at her face? Probably consider him crazy. And she'd damn well be right.

Tomorrow he was going to get the hell out of here and head back to Houston. If Trent was the man who'd gotten her pregnant, Jack couldn't help it. It was his nephew's problem. Not his. He was going to stay out of the whole mess.

"I kept myself occupied," he told her.

She opened the door without unlocking it and gestured for him to proceed her inside. The room was dusky dark. After a few steps, he waited for her to flip on a nearby lamp.

"You'll have to excuse the clutter," she told him. "I don't always have time to do my own housecleaning."

Jack glanced around the small living room. It was neat and cozy with just a few glasses and cups and papers scattered here and there. Although the furnishings were old and worn, nothing was dirty and he could see she'd made an effort to decorate the place with flowers and pictures and candles. It was very modest compared to his two-story home in the suburbs of Houston. But then, this house was truly lived in, whereas his was simply rooms decorated to look like a home.

"Where do you want me to put these things?" he asked.

"The books go on the desk in the corner. The groceries in the kitchen."

An antique roll-top desk sat near a window facing the beach. A breeze was blowing in through the open screen, making the heat inside the house not so unbearable.

Jack deposited the books next to the telephone, then followed her down a short hallway to the kitchen. The ceiling was low, the floor tiled. One wall facing the west was made up of windows that were all open to the breeze. It was far cooler in here than the living room.

"Do you know what's wrong with your air conditioner?" he asked as he placed the sack on the cabinet counter.

"No. I wish I could call a repairman, but that takes more money than I have at the moment. I'm just thankful the summer hasn't been all that bad."

In Jack's opinion the summer had been hot as hell, and he tried to imagine his last girlfriend pregnant and penniless, while trying to cope with everyday trials. The woman would be screaming and crying at the top of her lungs for someone to take care of her. Frankly, he couldn't understand how Grace was holding up under the strain.

"The heat can't be good for your condition," he commented.

She joined him at the countertop and began to pull the items from the grocery sack. "For hundreds of years women have gone through pregnancies without the aid of air-conditioning. Surely, I can, too."

But he didn't want Grace to have to suffer needlessly. The notion struck him so hard and fast he was fairly stunned by it. And where had it come from? He didn't know this woman. Not really. There was no telling what kind of misery she might be planning for his nephew.

"Well, I'd better be going," he said, even though he couldn't quite make himself take the first step to leave.

"I'm going to grill fish for my supper. You're welcome to join me, if you like," she invited. "I only have two fillets, but I'd be happy to share. Or if you want me to cook something for you later, I could come over to the bungalow."

This was the time for him to fess up, Jack thought. To tell her he was Trent's uncle and that he'd really offered her the job just to give him an opportunity to spy on her personal life. But something on her tired face stopped him.

Before he knew what he was doing, he heard himself saying, "I have plenty of steaks over at my place. I could bring them over."

A weary smile tilted the corners of her lips and Jack

thought she truly appeared to be happy at the idea of
having a dining companion. He felt like a heel. Then
just as quickly cursed himself for being soft.

"Only for yourself," she told him. "I'll eat the fish.
It's good for the baby."

The simple statement was enough to tell Jack she
loved the little life growing inside her. The idea sent
something strange and warm surging through him, but
he tried his best to ignore the unfamiliar feeling.

"Fine," Jack said to her. "I'll go change and be back
in a few minutes."

An idiot had more sense than he did, Jack told himself as he stepped beneath the spray of the shower. He
was forty years old. He had no business making friends
with Grace Holliday. For Trent's sake, or any other reason. He hadn't come to Biloxi for female companion-
ship. His last girlfriend had been no less of a viper than
the ones he'd had before. She'd either wanted sex or
money, or both, in monumental proportions. Once he'd
shaken loose of her, he'd come to the conclusion he
never wanted a woman in his life. He didn't care if he
ever bedded another one.

That thought brought him up short. Because he suddenly realized this strange excitement he felt when he
was around Grace had nothing to do with sex. Well,
practically nothing, he corrected himself. He simply
wanted to be near her. Hear her voice, look at her, talk
to her. Just the idea of sharing supper with her had set
his heart to pounding.

Dear God, this wasn't like him. It wasn't like him at

. . . g his face up to the hard-driving spray, he

stood for a full minute beneath the cool water and prayed his mind would clear.

Grace had told him she was carrying Trent's child. If that was true, nothing or no one could ever change the fact. He couldn't allow himself to be attracted to one of his nephew's castoffs. It didn't matter if she was beautiful or lonely or needy. Jack already had enough troubles without falling for a woman like Grace.

Chapter Four

Grace, you're a foolish girl, she told herself as she stripped off the rumpled clothing she'd worn all day, then stepped into a fresh, blue dress. Look where a man has already gotten you.

For a moment she forgot about closing the zipper as her hands cradled the mound of baby growing inside her. She didn't regret the child. She loved it fiercely, and always would. The only thing she mourned was that the boy or girl would never know its father.

Grace had been a fool to let her head be turned by Trent's smooth talk and flashy smile, but since her grandfather had passed away, she'd not had anyone to be close to either physically or emotionally.

She'd not planned for the dates she'd had with Trent to turn into anything serious, but he'd truly seemed to care about her and she'd lapped up his attention like a starving cat. Never stopping to think what the consequences might be.

Later, Trent had been horrified at the idea of being a

husband and father, and had made no bones about telling Grace so. He'd considered them both too young to be saddled with such responsibilities and had urged her to get an abortion. He'd never meant for their relationship to be that serious, anyway.

Grace hadn't bothered to remind him about all the times he'd promised to love her forever. In the end, she'd gladly let him off the hook. She didn't want anyone who didn't want her. And after she'd told him he needn't be concerned about her or the baby, he'd gone back to Texas, relieved that she hadn't tried to ruin his life just because they'd had sex together.

Trent's use of her had taught Grace a hard lesson. Still, she had to go on as best she could and make a good life for the baby. She was determined to give her child love, a settled home, and a sense of security. Something her mother had never given Grace.

When Jack knocked on the door a few minutes later, he was wearing a pair of Levi's jeans and a yellow polo shirt. His wet hair was slicked back form his forehead as though he'd showered, but the day-old growth of rusty-red whiskers still covered his face. Grace invited him back to the kitchen, certain she'd never seen a more sexy man in her life. He was so downright male, it made her breath catch to just look at him.

"I brought a few more things with the steak," he told her. "I didn't think you'd mind."

He handed her the brown paper sack he was carrying. Grace placed it on the small dinette table and peeked inside. "Oh! Fresh vegetables! I can make a salad, and there's corn on the cob, too! This is wonderful, Jack!"

He'd seen women not show this much excitement over a piece of diamond jewelry. It made him think she either desperately needed money for food or it didn't take much to make her happy.

"I'm glad you're pleased."

"Pleased!" She turned a bright smile on him. "Oh, you can't imagine how sick I get of eating canned food. Fresh vegetables and company, too. This is going to be a special night."

A special night.

The words rolled over in Jack's mind as he watched Grace carry the sack of food over to the cabinet counter. She wouldn't think it so special if she knew who he really was. But he couldn't tell her just yet. He had to think of Jillian and all the pain his sister might have to endure if Grace decided to make demands on Trent.

The whole idea filled him with revulsion and though he tried to shake the dark image away, it kept him quiet for so long that Grace eventually glanced over her shoulder at him.

"Is something wrong?" she asked.

He tried to smile, but he'd never been much good at it, anyway. The lopsided twist to his lips reflected his mood.

"No. Why?"

"You look like you have murder on your mind."

"Don't worry. I'm not a serial killer disguised as a lawyer," he said, then joined her at the cabinet counter. "What do you want me to do?"

His offer surprised Grace and for a moment she merely looked at him. "Nothing. Remember, I'm the one who's supposed to be doing the cooking for you."

The man in him wanted to believe she'd invited him to supper because she'd wanted his company not because she considered it her job to prepare him a meal.

"You didn't have to start the job tonight," he couldn't help saying.

The strange, searching look in his gray eyes forced her to drop her gaze to the steaks on the counter. "I know. I...just...you don't have to pay me for tonight. Consider this one free. Sort of a trial meal."

From the very start she hadn't tried to hide the fact that she needed money. Yet she was telling Jack she didn't want pay. That wasn't the way most women worked. But then, her plans could be to get a much bigger pot from Trent.

"If that's the case, I feel obliged to help. Just tell me what to do."

She glanced at him from the corner of her eye. His hair had started to dry into waves. An indefinable scent like rain in a mountain forest emanated from his skin and clothes. She could feel the warmth of his body and imagine the power of his broad shoulders.

Sucking in a deep breath, she let it out slowly, then purposely stepped away from him. "All right. I'd be very happy for you to light the grill. And then I'll let you choose whether you want to do the meat or vegetables."

In no time at all they had the simple meal put together. Grace insisted it was no trouble to carry everything out to the wooden table situated beneath the live oak, where the night air had grown balmy and much cooler than inside the kitchen.

"Mmm, this is so delicious," Grace commented as they began to eat. "I can't remember anything tasting so good." She cast him a pointed glance. "You told me last night you didn't cook. You grilled this fish perfectly."

From the opposite side of the small table Jack

watched the flickering light of nearby bamboo torches cast playful shadows across her face as she continued to dig into the flaky fish.

"I only cook when I have to," he replied, then added, "I thought pregnant women were always sick and throwing up."

She glanced at him, her expression full of quizzical humor. "Only a small percentage does that, and usually in the first months of pregnancy. But not me. I love to eat." She peered at him more closely. "Didn't you know that? I mean...well, you haven't ever had a child?"

The corners of his mouth turned downward as he sliced into his steak. "I told you I didn't have a family."

"I know...but I thought you might have a child. Somewhere."

Did she believe he was the same sort of guy that had fathered her child? A man who was only out for his own personal pleasure and to hell with anything else? He hated to think she had that opinion of him.

"I was married for five years, but she didn't want any children."

Grace's eyes widened ever so slightly, as though she were finding it difficult to imagine any woman not wanting a child. "You haven't married since?"

"Lenore divorced me ten years ago. Since then I've been single."

With a slight shake of her head, she asked, "Why didn't your ex-wife want children?"

He shrugged, hoping to give her the impression that she was stirring at dead ashes. "She was a career woman. She worked in advertising for a big hotel chain based in Houston. She wanted to climb to the top and stay there. Nurturing a child was not in her plans.''

"How sad. Is that why you divorced? Because you wanted children?''

At the time, the issue of a baby was one of the more minor problems between them. He'd married Lenore because he'd wanted someone to love and to have that someone love him back. He'd wanted a spouse to share his life with. Yet it hadn't taken him long to learn Lenore hadn't been interested in sharing, only acquiring. He supposed their divorce had been the turning point in his life. Her treatment of their marriage had hardened him and, down through the years, he'd grown even harder. It was easier, safer, to not give a damn.

"Back when we were first married I wanted a child. Particularly a boy." He'd wanted a son to raise in exactly the opposite way John Barrett had raised him. It would have been appeasement for Jack. "But that wasn't the main reason we divorced. She was from a well-to-do family in Houston. Social position was almost as important to her as money. After a while I reached the conclusion that I would never be able to give her enough to keep her happy.''

Frowning, Grace murmured, "Poor woman.''

His bark of laughter was full of mocking humor. "Poor woman! Lenore has money to burn. She has exactly what she wants.''

"I still feel sorry for her. She probably doesn't realize how miserable she really is.''

Jack reached for the long-necked beer he'd carried over from his house. "You're a strange girl, Grace Holliday.''

She caught his gaze with hers. "Why is that? Because I'm simple?''

Just when Jack thought he was beginning to figure this woman out, she threw him for another loop. "No. You seem very intelligent to me."

Grace shook her head. "I don't mean that sort of simple. I mean because I live an ordinary life. Especially compared to yours."

There was something about her eyes, Jack thought. Every time she leveled them on him, he felt the oddest emotions rush through him. Like a freight train with the throttle wide open and no brakes to stop it.

"How would you know how I live?" he asked, his voice full of sour humor.

Grace swallowed a mouthful of food before she answered. "You live in a very large city. You obviously have money and a high-powered career."

His eyes took their time surveying her smooth features. "You couldn't know about my career. I might be an ambulance chaser. For all you know, I have to beg for cases."

She giggled at that idea. "I sincerely doubt you've ever begged...for anything."

His brows lifted ever so slightly. "Is that so?"

"I'm sure of it. Success is written all over you. But I also have the notion it hasn't made you happy."

That she could read him so closely irritated the hell out of Jack. He didn't want to be an open book to anyone. Especially this woman.

"What would you know about happy?" he muttered the question as he sliced off another bite of steak.

A smooth, distant expression fell over her features. "For a while after my baby's father left, I thought I could never be happy again. But now—well, I want to believe the future will be better. I have to believe that—for the baby's sake."

If Trent was the father, Jack hated to think his nephew could be so callous and irresponsible. But then, for all Jack knew, Grace could have led Trent on, while assuring him she was on birth control.

"Are you certain the guy isn't coming back? There's a possibility he could have a change of heart, isn't there?" Jack suggested.

She let out a mocking laugh. "As soon as Trent discovered I was pregnant, he couldn't hightail it fast enough. I would be stunned if he ever showed his face around here again. Especially now that I've learned he's sold the bungalow to you."

Jack tried not to wince. She truly believed Trent had owned the bungalow and Jack had furthered the deception by telling Grace he'd bought it. He was beginning to wonder just where this whole subterfuge was going to end.

"So you…believe you'll never hear from him again?"

Sad shadows filled her green eyes, making Jack wonder if she had honestly loved Trent at one time. Or was she simply sad because her plan to acquire a rich husband had gone awry? Dear Lord, he wished he knew.

"No," she answered. "But that's all right. It would have been nice if he'd agreed to give the child fatherly attention. But not if it was done grudgingly. I don't want that. My baby deserves better."

Funny, but Jack expected he'd feel the same way if he were in Grace's shoes. "But what about money? The boy or girl is going to need things."

Her fork paused in midair as her lips compressed to a thin line. "I will take care of my child's needs, Jack. He or she might not be raised in the manner you were, but he won't be neglected."

Jack had been born into luxury and during his childhood he'd not wanted for anything. Except love from his mother and understanding from his father. In the end he'd gotten neither. Maybe if he had, he'd be a happy man today.

"I wasn't trying to imply otherwise, Grace. But it does take money to care for a child and you've already admitted you're stretched."

Her gaze firmly on her plate, she stabbed at the fish. "I don't plan on being poor forever."

"You plan on marrying a rich man?"

Her eyes lifted to stare a hole right through him. "If I ever agree to marry a man, it will be because I love him and trust him and believe that we'll be together forever."

She sounded so insulted, so resolute, Jack had to believe her. "And until then, what are you going to do?"

With a weary sigh, she leaned back in her chair. "I don't understand all these questions, Jack. I thought the job interview ended yesterday."

Jack knew he was asking too many questions, but in truth, he wanted to hurl just as many more at her.

Shrugging, he said as casually as he could, "It did. But I—I'm just curious about your plans. It's not often I run across a young pregnant woman trying to fend for herself."

Her nostrils flared. "No. In your social circle I'm sure you never run across anyone like me."

Grace believed her lack of money was the thing that differentiated her from the women he'd known. But actually it was much more. In spite of her condition, there was a fresh innocence about her, a sweetness that would be hard to feign.

"I don't *do* social circles, Grace. I don't have the

time or desire to drink cocktails and act as though I like people who are as phony as a three-dollar bill.''

She appeared surprised by his blunt statement. ''I figured that was a requirement that went along with your job. At least, that's my way your profession is portrayed in movies and books.''

''It takes more than social standing and outward appearances to impress me,'' he said flatly. If someone wants Jack Barrett to defend them, then they lay their cards out on the table and I say yes or no. It's that simple.''

She studied him over the rim of her glass. ''And is it safe for me to assume those cards you're talking about are bills? Like hundreds and thousands.''

Jack was suddenly seeing himself reflected in her eyes and he didn't like image at all. Dropping his gaze to the food on his plate, he said, ''You have a pretty low opinion of me, don't you?''

She tilted her head to one side as she continued to study him. ''Not entirely. I figure at one time in your life you were a nice, sensitive man. But through the years you've…learned not to care so much. About the law—your cases.''

She was right, Jack thought. In the early years after law school, he'd wanted to defend only the right and just, but his father had ridiculed his ideas, telling him if he wanted to be a success, he had to forget about balancing the scales of justice. In the real world there was no fairness. Only the tough survived to win the big piece of pie.

''If I had let myself care the way you think I should have, I would have already died of ulcers or a heart attack a long time ago.'' Instead he'd let his dreams die, along with his emotions.

From the other side of the table, Grace studied his glum face. Placing her glass back on the table, she asked, "Why did you really come to Biloxi, Jack?"

His gaze swiftly lifted to meet hers. "Why?" he repeated. "I told you. For rest."

"You appear to be very healthy and fit."

He frowned mockingly. "Thanks. For a man of forty, that's great to hear."

A smile briefly tilted the corners of her lips. "Don't tell me you think of yourself as old. That's ridiculous."

"You're a very young woman. You wouldn't know how I feel." In fact, Jack himself didn't know. In the past months he'd begun to fear he couldn't feel anything. But now as Grace's searching green eyes traveled over him, he realized he'd been very wrong. Reckless, indecent urges were pounding inside him like a pagan drumbeat in a far-off jungle.

"I told you. I'm twenty-three."

He swigged down another drink of beer. "You're just an infant."

Slowly, she put down her fork and rose to her feet. When Jack glanced up at her face, he could see it was tightly closed.

"I'm going after dessert," she told him.

He watched her go into the house, then with a silent groan, he banged his fist softly against the tabletop.

He didn't need this. Little by little he could feel himself being sucked into Grace's life. If he didn't make himself pack and leave in the morning, he didn't know what he might end up doing or saying. Things that might be irreversible. Things he might later regret.

But packing and heading to Houston wouldn't solve his problem, Jack argued with himself. Once he was back in Texas, he would still be thinking, wondering, about her and the baby. What she intended to do and how she was going to survive.

Damn it all, he cursed. Rising to his feet, he headed into the house to find her.

She was in the kitchen making coffee when he entered the room. As he approached her, she glanced up but didn't smile, and Jack felt foolishly disappointed.

"I've made you angry," he stated.

Without looking at him, she placed waffle cookies on a saucer.

"No. I'm not angry."

A step away from her, he leaned his hip against the cabinet counter and studied her bent head. Her black hair glistened like satin beneath the overhead light. It fell in curly waves upon her shoulders and he desperately wished for an excuse to touch it. And her.

"If you're not angry, what's wrong?"

She cast him a sidelong glance, then a soft sigh slipped past her lips. "I've been living here on my own since I was eighteen years old, Jack. It offends me to hear you call me an infant."

Something in his chest tightened. "I didn't mean you were incompetent. But you are an infant to me, Grace. You're just starting your life, whereas, I—I'm looking back. It's not a pleasant feeling, believe me."

Her teeth sank into the fullness of her lower lip as she glanced away from him. "Sometimes I get touchy for no reason. Being pregnant has done something to me. I apologize. I shouldn't have called you ridiculous."

"Yes. You had every right to," he said, "Because I am."

This brought her head back around and her eyes were full of questions as they met his. "Why?"

Bitter resignation twisted his features. "My doctor told me I needed rest from the office. But I think I really left Houston because I didn't like who and what I had become there. I thought being here would help, but a man can't run from his problems. And tonight...when you invited me to supper...I felt things I had no business feeling."

At least, for this one time, he was being honest with her, Jack thought.

Grace's breath lodged in her throat as she tried to assemble the meaning of his words. He couldn't be attracted to her. No. He was from a different world. And she was pregnant with another man's child.

As the percolator began to gurgle behind her, she turned to face him.

"Jack, are you...running away from a woman?"

No. He was running to one. As sure and straight as a deadly arrow. But he couldn't let himself, he continued to argue with himself. Grace was young. Not to mention pregnant. And possibly even conniving. Still, he wanted her as nothing he'd ever wanted before.

With a trembling hand, he reached for the lock of hair clinging to the side of her neck. "I wish it were that simple, Grace."

"All things are simple. If we let them be."

Her voice had turned husky. The allure of it tugged on Jack's senses. Before he could stop himself, his head was bending to hers.

Yesterday, when Grace had first met Jack and all through this evening, the wonder of what it might be like to kiss him had continued to tempt her thoughts. Now she couldn't step away as his lips gently covered hers. This was something she'd been craving. Now that she had it, she couldn't resist.

The searching pressure of his lips lasted no more than a few moments, but it was enough to scorch Grace's senses. For long seconds after he lifted his head, her eyes remained closed and her hand continued to clutch the front of his shirt.

"Grace."

The whisper of her name caused her eyes to finally flutter open. Quickly she stepped back and prayed he couldn't see the rapid throb of her heartbeat.

"Was that…a test?" she asked.

His gray eyes swept over her face until they eventually settled on the lips he'd just kissed.

"No. It was a mistake."

She let out a shaky breath. "Why?"

"Because I want to do it again."

Chapter Five

"At least you're an honest man, Jack."

But that didn't mean she ought to be kissing him again, Grace thought. No. That one taste of him had shook her all the way to the soles of her feet. She couldn't let herself think about what two might do to her. She had to make light of it all. Because she knew the kiss had been nothing more than a physical, impulsive urge on his part.

Turning his head away from her, Jack wiped a weary hand over his face. "You're wrong about me, Grace. I'm hardly an honest man."

An amused smile tilted her lips. "So you were lying about wanting to kiss me again?"

Jack wished to hell he'd been lying. About that, at least. When he spoke, frustration made his voice gruff. "Any man would want to kiss you more than once."

The smile on her face deepened. "It's not necessary to be so kind, Jack. I'm well aware that I look like a ripe pumpkin."

"I wasn't talking about…well, I'm a lawyer. Doesn't that say enough about me?"

Her smile faded as she studied the grim expression on his face. Obviously he deeply regretted kissing her. The idea hurt. Though she didn't understand why. Jack Barrett wasn't anything to her. Just a next-door neighbor and a temporary one, at that.

"You said a lawyer's job was to pull the focus of attention away from the real issue. I wouldn't equate that with lying."

Why did she have to be so damn nice? Jack wondered. Why wasn't she showing him the scheming, sly woman he expected her to be? It would make this whole thing so much easier on him and his conscience.

"And I wouldn't necessarily say you look like a ripe pumpkin."

Something in his eyes warmed and softened. The look disturbed Grace because it matched the needy feeling simmering inside her.

Quickly she stepped around him and headed to the door leading out to the backyard. "I—I think I'd better go clear the table," she told him. "Help yourself to coffee and cookies."

Before she could take two steps, his hand came down on her shoulder. She paused as heat from his fingers radiated up her neck and filled her cheeks with color. Embarrassed by the reaction, she could hardly bring herself to glance up at him. When she did, her expression was questioning.

"I'll clear the table," he said. "You have dessert."

"I'm supposed to be working for you, Jack. Remember?"

He remembered all too much, Jack thought. The feel of her skin, the taste of her lips, the seductive scent of her. But most of all, he couldn't forget she was with child. His nephew's child.

"Tonight doesn't count. There'll be time enough to see my slave-driving ways."

The little grin on her lips said she'd never believe he could be a slave driver. It reminded Jack of all the times he'd forced Irene to work into the night. His secretary had often complained that she had a life outside the office, but Jack had never cared about Irene's needs. Being prepared for the next case was all that mattered to him.

"I don't imagine your employees do much complaining," Grace said.

A subtle smile twisted his lips. "Not when they're afraid to."

He dropped his hand, then went out the door, leaving Grace staring after him.

After three trips, he had everything back in the kitchen. When he began to wash the dishes, Grace quickly rose to her feet and joined him at the double sink.

"Leave the dishes," she told him. "I'll wash them later."

Jack should leave more than the dishes. If he'd been smart he would have gotten out of here long before he'd been an idiot and let himself kiss the woman. But he could see how weary she was. If he could keep her off her feet a few minutes, it would help make him feel a little less guilty.

"Look, Grace, I don't feel this generous too often. Just indulge me for once. Sit down. And when I have the dishes washed and dried, you can put everything away."

The expression on her soft features said she wanted

to argue. Jack released the sudsy plate back into the water, took her by the arm and set her down in one of the dinette chairs.

"Eat your dessert," he gently commanded.

"I don't need it."

"The baby probably does."

That was enough to make her lift one of the cookies to her mouth. Satisfied she would stay put, Jack went back to his task at the sink.

"You haven't had any dessert," she pointed out.

"I'm full. I couldn't hold another bite."

"I'm glad," she replied. "I was afraid I'd forgotten what it's like to cook for two."

The dishcloth paused its circular motion around the plate as Jack digested her words. The idea of her cooking for some other man, even Trent, rubbed him raw. Which was silly. He'd never thought of any woman, including Lenore, in such an old-fashioned way. But the truth was, Jack had never had a woman do domestic things for him, unless she was getting paid for it. He'd never had a woman cook a meal just for him and just because she wanted to please him.

"Did you...make meals for Trent?"

"Not really. He was a junk-food eater." She wrinkled her nose as she sipped her coffee. "Actually, the more I think about it, the more I can see he and I were nothing alike."

"Then why did you become involved with him in the first place?"

She didn't answer immediately and Jack glanced over his shoulder to see she was in deep reflection as she gazed absently at some spot across the room.

"I've asked myself that same question a thousand

times. But in the end, I guess I was just lonely and he...seemed to really care."

The dishes forgotten for a moment, Jack turned to face her. "You're a beautiful young woman, Grace. I can't imagine you being lonely."

She frowned as she brought her gaze around to his. "Oh, I have friends and acquaintances. But that's not the same. Ever since Granddaddy died, I've felt lost. I suppose I was thinking Trent would fill the void." She snorted with self-contempt. "What a fool I was."

Her answers weren't those of a woman after a rich husband. But then, he'd be a crazy man to expect her to admit to such a thing, to confess that she'd been after Trent so she could live the rest of her life in luxury.

Turning back to the sinkful of dishes, he said with measured casualness, "You mentioned your grandfather. Did you live with him or something?"

"Since I was thirteen. My grandmother had already passed away by then. Elias, my granddaddy, died just after I turned eighteen. He was eighty by then and in pretty frail health. I think he hung on just to see me celebrate my birthday. This was his house. He'd lived here since he was a small child. Before he died, he gave it to me."

Jack could tell how much that meant to her. Pride and deep affection filled her voice.

"You must have been very close to him."

"I loved him more than anything," she admitted. "You see, he was the only family I had that really cared anything about me. My mother is...she never was too much of a parent. She's been married five times. I couldn't tell you what state she's living in now. Nevada, I believe. It's been more than a year since I've heard from her and I haven't actually seen her since Grand-daddy's funeral five years ago.''

My mother doesn't know about my pregnancy.

Jack had figured Grace had deliberately kept the fact from her mother. Now he knew the real reason. Grace more or less didn't have a mother.

"Why does she stay away? Do you two not get along?"

"She understands I don't particularly approve of her life-style, but we don't fuss and fight, if that's what you mean," Grace told him. "Basically she goes her way and forgets she has a daughter."

Once again, Jack glanced over his shoulder to look at her. "That must hurt you."

Her lips twisted with bitter acceptance. "When I was very small it did. Especially when she would drop me off at friend's or distant relative's and leave me there for weeks at a time. But now—well, I don't let myself think about her too much. And anyway, Jenny—that's my mother's name—has problems of her own. Problems she most likely won't ever get over."

"What sort of problems? With the law?"

Her expression dour, Grace shook her head. "No. I guess you would call them psychological. As for myself, I never could understand her behavior. But Grand-daddy always said Jenny would have been a different woman if my father hadn't been killed. He said she really, really loved him and his death sent her over the edge. She could never get over it."

"Maybe that's why she's had all those husbands," Jack reasoned. "She was trying to replace him."

Grace sighed. "I think she doesn't want to be around me because I remind her too much of her life with my father. I guess the sight of me is just too painful."

Resentment roiled inside him. He knew what it was like to be ignored and neglected. As a child Grace had no doubt endured the same pain and loneliness he'd felt. She hadn't deserved that. No one did.

Scrubbing at a fistful of silverware, he said bluntly, "I never see my mother. Nor do I want to."

She came to stand beside him and Jack could feel her searching gaze on the side of his face. "Why? Are you two estranged?"

Jack never talked about Francine. Even when Jillian brought up the subject of their mother, he would steer the conversation elsewhere. Her neglect had left hard scars inside him that he didn't want anyone knowing about. Yet here he was giving Grace a glimpse of that private part of him.

"That would be a nice way to put it," he answered. "She never cared about me or my sister. To her we were simply a nuisance, the dreaded aftereffects of sex. She divorced my father shortly before he died of a heart attack. Since then, she's stayed out of my life and I hers."

There was no mistaking the bitterness in his voice and Grace was amazed at how much it hurt to think of this man as a child, needing and wanting a mother who didn't return his love. "Maybe this time away has made her regret the way she treated you," Grace suggested.

He made a mocking sound deep in his throat. "It's too late for amends, Grace. I don't want them or need them. Not now."

She picked up the silverware he'd rinsed and began to dry it. "What about your father? Were you close to him?"

Too close, Jack thought. Because his father had given him love and attention, he'd adored and looked up to the man. All his young life, he'd done everything the old man had ever wanted just to make John Barrett proud. Even to this day, the powerful hold his father had over him was still too strong to allow Jack to let go of the firm.

"Yes, we were close. He was good to me in many ways. But I made the mistake of thinking he was some sort of god and could do no wrong."

"Every child wants to believe their parents can do no wrong."

"But they do," Jack said.

She sighed. "Yes. And I suppose I will, too. But I'm going to try very hard to do the right thing and make the best choices. Above anything, I want this child to be happy."

When Jack had first met this woman, all he could think about was finding out just how much money she planned to demand from Trent and what, if anything, he could do about it. All of his concerns had been for his nephew. But now he was beginning to wonder more and more about Grace and the baby. What could she do? How was she going to provide for the both of them?

"How much more college do you need before you can do whatever it is you're going to do?"

All the dishes were washed. Jack pulled the stopper and rinsed the sink while Grace put the last of the things away.

"If I didn't have to take time off to have the baby, I would get my degree at the midterm break in December. But now I'll have to go a little more in the spring."

"What sort of degree are you working toward?"

A wide smile suddenly spread across her face and Jack realized he'd touched on a subject close to her heart.

"I'm going to be a music teacher. I want to teach violin at a school where the arts are appreciated and stressed upon."

"And where will that be?" he wondered out aloud. "A private school?"

Her face wrinkled with doubt. "I'm not sure yet. I'd really rather it be public. Where all types of students get a chance to learn music."

"Most public schools just have band," he felt inclined to point out. "They don't include stringed instruments."

"Sadly, that's true. So I'll move to the east or west coast if necessary."

"And leave this place?"

"I would hate to," Grace admitted, "but that's the way I plan to make a living."

She filled a cup from the percolator and handed it to Jack, then picked up her own mug from the small dinette table. "Would you rather drink this outside where it's cooler?"

Now that the mess from the meal had been cleaned away, Jack had no real reason to stay. Except that he wanted to.

"You've had a long day and you're tired," he said.

"I'm okay. But don't let me keep you if you have something else to do."

She was letting him decide as to whether he wanted to stay or go. That was something new for Jack. His ex-wife and all the girlfriends he'd had over the years had expected, even demanded, that he follow their wants.

"Okay. I'll drink my coffee outside, then I'll head back to the bungalow," he told her.

She smiled as though she'd won a small victory. Jack

didn't like the idea. He had to view Grace as a case, a case he couldn't lose.

Under the live oak, the two of them sipped their coffee in mutual silence. A few miles to the east, lights of downtown Biloxi flickered through the trees, but thankfully they were far enough away to miss the noise of the traffic traveling up and down the casino strip.

After a while Jack said, "I saw you leave early this morning. Were you going to clean someone's house?"

Had he been watching or just happened to look out and see her car gone from the driveway? It didn't matter, she quickly reminded herself. Jack would only be here for a few days. Still, the idea of a man like him taking notice of her was rather intoxicating.

"Actually, I drove to the university in Hattiesburg to use the library. I had a lot of research to do on a paper I'm writing for a theory class."

His expression turned incredulous. "You drove all the way to Hattiesburg and back? That has to be eighty or ninety miles one way."

"That's right. But that's where the University of Southern Mississippi is located. I commute back and forth three days a week to class. Sometimes more."

He started to ask her why she didn't stay in Hattiesburg during school term, but the answer quickly came to him before he got the question out. She'd already admitted she was pinching pennies just to survive. She didn't have the finances to pay for extra housing.

"The drive gets to be tiring," she went on, "but housing there would be a big cost. And I don't ever want to get rid of this place. Even if I don't always live here in the future, it will make a good summer home."

That she was sentimental about this place didn't surprise Jack. It appeared to be all she had. It and her baby.

Damn it, Jack, he chided himself, there isn't any reason to get soppy about it. She's a young, intelligent, able-bodied woman. She won't always be in this situation. No doubt, some man will soon come along and make her life easy. Some man who would be only too eager to give this woman everything she needs and wants.

The notion left him feeling as if he'd eaten a plate of nails for supper. Trying to ignore the clawing in his gut, he glanced her way, then watched in silent fascination as she shook her hair back from her face and propped her bare feet on a nearby chair. Immediately, Jack's gaze zeroed in on her red toenails then traveled over her ankles and up to where the hem of her blue dress stopped in the middle of her calves.

He was wondering just how soft her skin would feel beneath his hand when she asked, "What kind of lawyer are you?"

Jack forced his gaze to move to her face. "A trial lawyer. My firm handles cases for major companies that are either being sued or seeking a settlement."

She nibbled at the cookie in her hand. "Oh. I thought you might be a criminal lawyer. You seem more like that sort."

Funny she could see that about him, whereas none of his family had, Jack thought. John Barrett had considered criminal law seedy and not good enough for his son to practice.

"My father and his father before him were corporate lawyers. I didn't want to break the tradition."

She searched his face for long moments. "Didn't want to? Or just couldn't?"

His eyes fell to the cup in his hand. There were only two more swallows and then he needed to go.

"My older sister wasn't lawyer material, so that left me the responsibility of keeping the firm going."

"You could have changed the type of cases it handled."

He let out a short, caustic laugh. "It's not that easy, Grace."

She grimaced. "Well, I understand you think I'm naive. But I happen to believe what I told you earlier. Things are simple if we let them be."

He swallowed the remainder of his coffee and set the cup on the table. "You know, I do believe I'm going to miss talking to you once I'm gone," he admitted.

A strange dread settled over Grace as she shot him an anxious glance. "Are you leaving soon?"

"I don't know," he said roughly. "Maybe tomorrow. Or the next day. I really should get back." But the idea of never seeing this woman again was giving him a great deal of trouble. And not because of what she might do to Trent once he was gone.

"You have cases waiting on you?" she asked.

"Always."

"You have other lawyers to help you?"

"Plenty. It's a big firm."

"Then why not let them do it for a while?" she suggested. "I'll bet it's been a long time since you've lain on the beach and watched the clouds and the birds, or read a book."

"I read briefs and depositions all the time."

She wrinkled her nose. "That isn't anything like fiction."

And she wasn't anything like he'd imagined she would be. He was feeling things toward her he'd never expected to feel. For the first time he could ever remember, he wasn't in control of a situation. Or himself.

"It's getting late," he said, rising to his feet.

She joined him and they walked back to the house together. Inside, she followed him to the front door and thanked him for the vegetables and his company.

Jack stepped onto the front porch, then glanced at her as she stood in the open doorway. "Grace, about that kiss—I hope you didn't think anything about it."

Even though he stood in the darkness, she studied the silhouette of his face for what felt like an eternity. "Of course I didn't. I'm not nearly as naive as you keep thinking."

He looked out toward the ocean. It was calm now and to the east a yellow moon was just rising, glistening the water with gold ribbons of satin. It was a beautiful sight, he thought, but not nearly as mesmerizing as the woman standing behind him.

"I don't exactly go around kissing women on impulse. I mean, women I've just met."

"Forget it, Jack. It's not like I have a daddy standing to one side with a shotgun. If that was the case, Trent would have been in trouble a long time ago."

But Trent was no longer here. It was Jack who was now falling for Grace. And falling into trouble.

"I won't let it happen again," he promised, more to himself than to her.

She tried to tell herself to not be hurt. The man was only being sensible. She and Jack Barrett had no business kissing. Now or ever. But the idea left her feeling hollow just the same.

"I'm sure you won't," she said, her voice husky as she pushed the words through her tight throat. "Good night, Jack."

"Good night," he murmured, then, stepping off the porch, he strode off toward the shadows and the bungalow next door.

Chapter Six

The next day was the start of the weekend and Grace always did Miss Kate's laundry on Saturday morning. The old woman was somewhat of a fixture in the area, living eighty-five years in the same spot only a few blocks from Grace. She'd been friends with her grandfather and though he'd tried to marry her long before he'd passed away, Kate had refused, vowing she liked her independence better than men. But Grace understood the woman was still in love with her husband, who'd been killed in the Pacific Islands in World War II.

Over the years Grace's visits to Kate's house had become more than a job. The old woman had become a second grandmother to her and in turn, Kate treated Grace as a grandchild of her own. She would never dream of allowing Grace to get straight to the business of laundry. Instead, Grace always had to go through the ritual of fixing the old woman a glass of iced tea with lemon and playing her at least two songs on the violin. Kate would be satisfied with nothing less.

"Miss, Kate, how many times have I told you," Grace gently admonished the little white-haired lady sitting in an oak rocker on the back porch, "you pay me to do your laundry. Not play the violin."

Kate waved her bony hand in protest. "I ain't a bit worried about the laundry, honey. I can take care of it myself if I have to. But I can't hear Betty's waltz played on the fiddle just any day of the week. Now mind me, girl, and play it for an old woman."

Grace leaned forward in the wicker chair and pulled her instrument from the case lying at her feet. After plucking the strings to make sure it was in tune, she played Kate's request.

As the slow, sweet notes of the waltz filtered out over the back porch, the old woman closed her eyes and smiled with fond remembrance.

"Bob Wills couldn't have done it better, my girl. And I know, 'cause me and Walter went to see him and his Texas playboys one time over in Mobile."

Because Grace had heard the story before, she smiled with patient affection. "Really? Did you dance?"

Kate chuckled. "Oh, my. Every dance. 'Til two in the morning. But I was young then. Like you. Young and pretty." She sighed wistfully, then pointed a bent finger at Grace. "Now play the 'Goodnight Waltz' and I'll let you be."

Grace played the second waltz, repeating several sections to give her friend a few more moments of pleasure. Once she put down her instrument, she shot Kate a sly smile. "You'd think you had romance on your mind, wanting to hear waltzes today. Have you found a fella I don't know about?"

Kate snorted as she reached for her tea. "I'm too old to have a man sniffin' around my neck."

"But you're still very beautiful. I know Granddaddy thought so."

Kate's tight lips relaxed into a smile. "Your grand-daddy's heart was too soft. Just like yours." She eyed Grace with a keen brown eye. "How's the baby?"

"Kicking strong. The doctor says only about four weeks now."

Kate nodded with approval, then her face wrinkled into a frown. "Guess you haven't heard from that no-account fella?"

Grace shook her head. "No, ma'am. The other night I thought he'd come back. The lights were on in the bungalow, but it turns out someone else has bought the place."

Kate sniffed as she digested Grace's news. "Guess that means he don't plan on comin' back."

"No," Grace quietly agreed. "He won't come back. But I did get a job out of the new owner," she added brightly. "I haven't really started yet. But I'm hoping he'll have something for me to do today."

One of Kate's thin white eyebrows lifted with wry speculation. "It's another man that's moved in?"

"Yes. A lawyer from Houston."

"He's a rich Texan," she stated rather than asked. "Does he have a family?"

Grace shook her head. "He told me he was divorced."

"How old is he?"

"Forty."

Kate clucked her tongue with disapproval. "That's a bad age. A man's a handsome devil at that age. But it's a time when his head gets messed up. He's lived a lot and knows a lot. But not nearly enough to know it all. You know what I mean?"

Grace looked at the old woman as she thought about Jack and the troubled shadows she sometimes saw in his gray eyes. "I think so."

Kate shook her crooked forefinger at Grace. "Mind yourself, girl. He might start looking across the fence at you."

Grace laughed. "Miss Kate, I'm about to have a baby. No man is going to look at me the way you're thinking."

Kate snorted again. "That mound of baby don't make you ugly, honey. Just makes you look good and fertile."

Grace bent forward and placed her violin and bow back in the case, then, rising to her feet, she said, "You don't have to worry about me, Miss Kate. This man doesn't care anything about finding a fertile woman. He doesn't even want a wife, much less a child."

"Humph. Sounds worse than the one before."

Suddenly Grace was remembering the feel of Jack's lips, the scent of him, the mindless pleasure those few moments of kissing him had given her. In spite of the heat on the porch, she came close to shivering.

"You might very well be right, Miss Kate."

Later that afternoon Jack wiped the sweat from his brow and glanced furtively around Grace's backyard. It was a good thing there weren't any close neighbors around them. Otherwise they would have already suspected him of burglarizing the place.

He probably shouldn't have taken it upon himself to go inside her house, but there was no other way to get to the thermostat that controlled the air-conditioning unit. He'd discovered a loose electrical wire and now that he'd restored a tight connection, the thing appeared to be running and cooling normally.

He was glad he'd gotten the work finished before Grace came home. No doubt she would have argued, telling him it wasn't his place to work on her air conditioner. And maybe it wasn't. Lord only knew he shouldn't be doing anything that would drag him further into her life. But last night in his nice, cool bedroom, he'd lain awake for a long time, wondering how Grace could possibly sleep in the muggy heat. Especially when her condition only allowed her to lay in limited positions.

Why that should bother him, Jack didn't know. It wasn't his fault the woman was pregnant or without money. He wasn't her keeper. And he shouldn't be poking his nose into her business. Even if Trent was the father of her baby.

Still, he wasn't completely satisfied her future plans were to dismiss Trent entirely from his responsibilities as the baby's father. Sure, she seemed gentle, kind, even uninterested in wealth, as far as the sort the Barretts's possessed. But how would she be once the baby was here and its care put demands on her already strained pocketbook?

What are you going to do, Jack? Hang around here until the baby is born just to find out who and where she's going to turn to for money? He couldn't. He had a job, a life of his own. Such as it was.

Jerking his sweaty T-shirt over his head, Jack left Grace's backyard and headed for the bungalow. Inside, he pulled a long-necked bottle of beer from the small refrigerator and took a healthy swig of the cold brew.

Before he could a take a second drink however, the cell phone he'd brought along with him rang. Not many people had the private number. Only Irene, his sister Jillian, and a couple of associates. The call could be important.

He directed his steps toward the living room. When he answered, Irene's voice came back in his ear. "What have you been doing, Jack? You're never away from the phone."

"Remember, I came down here to get away from them," he was quick to remind her. "I only answered because I thought it might be an emergency."

His secretary laughed. "It was an emergency to make sure you're still alive."

He grimaced. "Why wouldn't I be?"

"I've tried to call you several times today and you didn't answer."

"I've been busy."

"You mean, ignoring the phone?"

"No. I mean out of the house. Away from the phone." He wasn't about to tell her what he'd really been doing. She'd probably laugh. Or even worse, point out what an idiot he was for allowing his head to be turned by a pregnant woman seventeen years younger than him.

"Well, sorry I interrupted, but I've been worried about you ever since I talked to you yesterday."

"It's Saturday, Irene, aren't you home?"

She paused for long seconds, then laughed with disbelief. "Since when have I ever had the time to take Saturdays off? I'm up to my elbows in work here."

He frowned, took a long drink of beer, then said, "Forget it, Irene. Go home and do whatever you want."

"Jack! Have you forgotten the tire company case will be coming up soon? You wanted all that information typed and ready when you got back here. And the liability case with the pharmaceutical company, you know the research on it is staggering—even with your partners taking on part of the work.''

"You have clerical people there to help you," he reminded her.

"Not enough."

"Then hire some temps. Or hire two or three permanently."

"On my own? I don't have the authority."

"I'm giving it to you."

Irene heaved out a breath and Jack could picture her wiry, hundred-pound frame as she flopped back against the desk chair. Her face was far more wrinkled than it should be, but she'd smoked like a chimney since an early age. Thankfully, she'd quit the habit five years ago and Jack didn't worry so much about her health now.

The idea stopped him short. It was strange, he'd never realized how much he'd worried about Irene or how he'd taken her devotion to him for granted until he'd met Grace.

"Jack, have you gone swimming and stepped on a jellyfish or something poisonous? I'm really beginning to think you're ill with a fever."

"I'm not ill, Irene. I've either been crazy for the past forty years or I've gone off the beam now. I don't know which. But it doesn't matter. Just do as I say. Go home. Quit worrying about Barrett, Winslow and Layton."

"Have you?"

For the time being Jack had put the firm totally out of his mind. For the past two and a half days Grace was all he'd been able to think about. Which was no doubt bad. But being obsessed with her could hardly be any worse than being controlled by his job. Or could it? he wondered.

"For the next few days I have. As for you, when Monday gets here, I want you to hire more help and offer them whatever salary you think is worthy. And give yourself a five-hundred-dollar raise."

"A month?" she asked in shock.

This time Jack chuckled. "That's what I said."

"All right, I'm not going to argue about that one," she said slowly. "Is there anything else you want me to take care of?"

Jack thought for a moment. "Yeah. Give me Jillian's phone number."

"You don't know your own sister's phone number," she said with disapproval. "You ought to be ashamed, Jack."

Jack grimaced. "There's lots of things I ought to be ashamed about. But Jillian knows I love her." After all, when it came right down to it, he wasn't going on with this subterfuge for Trent. He was beginning to believe the young man didn't deserve anything but a swift kick in the ass. No, he was doing all this for Jillian's sake. His sister had already endured a mountain of pain in her lifetime. If at all possible, Jack was determined to shield her as best he could from any more heartache.

Irene read the number off to him. He scribbled it down on a notepad lying beside the telephone, then, ending the conversation, he sat down with his beer.

By the time the bottle was empty, he still hadn't come up with a reason to call his sister without making her suspicious that something was wrong. The only feasible excuse he could come up with was that he was on vacation and had a little extra time to chat with her. But even that would sound suspicious to Jillian, who knew her brother never took vacations.

A knock at the door suddenly broke into Jack's thoughts. Rising to his feet, he crossed the small room and quickly opened the door. To find Grace on the other side of the threshold was not a huge surprise, but his immediate reaction to her was. The sight of her actually jolted him like a lightening bolt.

"Hello, Grace."

She merely looked at him with raised brows. "Would you mind telling me what you think you're doing?"

He stared back at her. "Drinking a beer. Does that offend you?"

She rolled her eyes and pressed her lips together. "No. And don't play dumb. You know what I'm talking about."

Jack opened the door and motioned for her to enter the bungalow. Grace hesitated for only a moment, then stepped past him and into the small living room.

Not until he'd closed the door behind him and turned to face her, did she notice he was wearing only jeans and a scruffy pair of tennis shoes. Like a magnet, her gaze was drawn to his bare chest, which was even more broad and muscled than she'd imagined it might be. Soft, russet hair fuzzed the area between two dark flat nipples, while lower, his abdomen was lean and hard.

Swallowing, she turned her head and tried to tell herself she really didn't have the urge to run her palms over his warm flesh or tangle her fingers in the hair on his chest. She'd be crazy to let herself want this man. Much less to act upon her feelings.

"Would you like something to drink?" he asked.

She glanced back at him. "No, thank you. I only

want to know why you—well, considered it okay to play repairman with my air conditioner?''

He grinned at her. "You don't like feeling cool?"

She made a helpless gesture with her hand. "Of course I do. It *feels* wonderful. But that's not the point."

He waved away her words as he headed toward the kitchen. Grace was forced to follow him.

"It's the only point," he said as he pulled another beer from the refrigerator. "The thing wasn't doing you any good as it was. Now it is. What's wrong with that?"

"Okay," she said with a goodly amount of exasperation. "Then give me the bill. I'll pay it somehow."

Jack twisted the lid on the bottle as he turned to face her. "There is no bill, Grace. I repaired the thing myself."

Her brows disappeared beneath the damp wisps of bangs on her forehead. "*You* repaired it! Have you been lying to me?"

The beer bottle paused halfway to his lips and for a moment his heart went stone still. "What do you mean lying?"

Grimacing, she shook her head. "You said you were a lawyer. Not a refrigerant repairman."

Relief flooded through him, making his shoulders visibly sag. "I am a lawyer, but that doesn't mean I'm totally incompetent about mechanical things."

She looked anything but convinced, and he said, "I had a good friend in college who was a genius with cars, motors, anything mechanical or electrical. I learned a lot by hanging out in his garage."

Grace's expression was suddenly mocking. "I'd rather think you were learning more about girls back then, than anything to do with motors."

Jack grinned. "I'd already learned all I needed to know about that."

"Really?"

His grin deepened and Grace felt her breath catch just a little at the sight of his even white teeth.

"Yeah. I knew if I didn't want to get into trouble, to stay away from them."

She was struggling to keep her mind on the issue at hand. "If you learned that much then you should have also learned that poking your nose into a woman's personal life will also get you into trouble."

He shot her a look of mocking disbelief. "Personal life? Come on, we're talking about sticking two wires back together, not sifting through your intimate diary."

"I have no diary," she said curtly.

"You understand my point," he countered knowingly.

She huffed out another heavy breath. "Yes, but you need to understand it was *my* air conditioner. You had no right to take it upon yourself to fix it!"

"Well excuse me for trying to be nice," he drawled sarcastically. Deliberately ignoring her, Jack tilted the bottle to his lips and swallowed half the contents.

"I didn't ask you to be nice!" she retorted, "but now—"

Her words broke off abruptly and Jack watched her head twist to one side and her teeth sink deeply into her bottom lip. She was more than angry with him, he realized, and for the life of him, he couldn't understand why.

"What? What now?"

She shot him a sidelong glance full of accusation. "Well, there's nothing left for me to do but pay you for making the repairs."

Stunned, his jaw dropped, then just as quickly tightened to granite as insult poured through him. "Like hell
you will."

"I won't have it any other way," she said flatly.

"You're crazy, woman! I put two wires together and
tightened a screw. Big deal. I don't want payment. I
didn't do it for payment."

"They why did you do it?"

She would have to ask something he didn't want to
answer. Even to himself. And as he studied her angry
face, all sorts of answers rolled through Jack's mind,
but in the end, he could only give her the truth.

"Because I don't want you being hot and miserable.
Especially at night when you're trying to sleep. Does
that make me bad in your eyes?"

No, Grace thought miserably, it made him anything
but bad. And suddenly she couldn't bear to face him.
Tears were already filling her eyes and clogging her
throat. Before she could let him see her burst into sobs,
she whirled and rushed out of the house.

Cursing, Jack tossed the remains of his beer into the
trash, then raked both hands over his hair. Damn it, if
he'd asked Grace's permission to check out the air conditioner first, she would have refused. So he'd done it
on his own. Because ultimately he'd figured she would
be pleased and grateful that he'd bothered. Instead, she
was furious.

He paced around the tiny kitchen for only a few seconds, then muttering another curse word, headed out the
door and across the yard to Grace's house.

He found her in the kitchen, her head lying on her
forearms, which were folded upon the tabletop. Her
shoulders were gently shaking with silent sobs.

She hadn't heard him come in and for a moment, Jack

could only stand in the open doorway, staring at her as a strange mix of feelings twisted through him. If he had a nickel for every time he'd seen a woman shed tears on the witness stand and in his private life, he'd be an even richer man than he was today. And down through the years, he'd grown indifferent to the emotional sprinklers that were turned on whenever sympathy or self-gain was wanted. Lenore had been great at it. Even his hard-boiled mother had been good at producing the waterworks when things weren't going to suit her.

But it was different with Grace. She'd not wanted Jack to see her tears. She was crying because something was really hurting her. And he hated to think that something was him.

Walking quietly up behind her, he placed his hand on the back of her shiny black hair. "Grace, what's wrong?"

She quickly reared her head up from the table and twisted her face far enough around to see him. "Why are you here? Haven't you done enough for one day?"

Her voice quivered with tears and lingering resentment. Her beautiful green eyes were red, the skin around them splotched and puffy.

"Do you want me to apologize?" he asked gently.

"No. It's too late for that. You've ruined everything."

Her hair felt soft and silky beneath his fingers. Before he could stop himself, he was stroking his hand down the long length lying against her back.

"Why is that, Grace? You're going to have to explain, because frankly, I don't understand."

The fact that he was touching her and it felt so good, so sweet, filled Grace with even more torment. Making a fool of herself over Trent had been one thing, but falling for Jack Barrett would make her even crazier than her fickle mother.

She gulped in a deep, bracing breath, then said in a voice rough with tears, "Because I don't want to be beholden. To you. Or any man."

This raised his eyebrows. "I don't want you to be beholden to me. That wasn't my intention. I was just trying to help you."

Pain stabbed at her too soft heart, making a fresh batch of tears rush to the backs of her eyes. Blinking furiously, she glanced away from him. "I don't want to be helped. Not by a man," she added bitterly.

"You asked me for a job," he gently reminded her. "Isn't that sort of the same thing?"

"No. That's compensation for my labor."

He let out a rough sigh. "In other words, it's okay for you to work for a man. But you're too proud to accept his help. Is that it?"

She wiped the back of her hand against her eyes and Jack was suddenly overwhelmed with the urge to pull her into his arms, to kiss each teardrop from her cheeks. God help him, he didn't want this woman to hurt. For any reason.

"I'm not too proud, Jack. But I—learned a lesson from Trent. Men always expect something in return for even the smallest favor. Their actions always have their own self-interest at heart."

Her words nettled him, making his voice sharp when he spoke, "I don't want or expect anything from you."

But he did, Jack guiltily reminded himself. He wanted information and answers. She would hate him if she only knew his secret.

"Maybe not," she said wearily. "But I can't work for you now. It wouldn't be right."

His forefinger wound itself around a strand of her hair and it was all Jack could do to keep from tugging on it, forcing her to rise from the chair so that he could take her in his arms. "Why?"

Aghast, she glanced up at him. "I could hardly take pay from you, if you won't accept it from me."

That she wanted to keep everything strictly business between them gouged at Jack even more. He didn't want them to be employee and employer. He wanted them to be more. Much more.

Like what? Friends? Lovers? They couldn't be. Once she discovered he was Trent's uncle there wouldn't be anything between them. It would all be over. And anyway, the idea was crazy! He didn't want a woman in any form or fashion.

"Okay, Grace. I worked for thirty minutes. So give me ten dollars. Will that make you happy?"

Did he honestly want her to be happy? Grace wondered. Since her grandfather died, she couldn't think of anyone who'd ever been truly concerned about her happiness . Unless it was Miss Kate. She cared. But Miss Kate wasn't anything like Jack Barrett.

Rising to her feet, she tried to smile at him, but it was wobbly at best. "Yes. But it isn't a fair price."

His lips twisted. "I don't have an electrician's license so I can't charge union wage. And since it takes about fifteen steps to get over here, I can't charge for a service call, either. Ten dollars is a fair price."

Her eyes searched his for long moments, making Jack wonder if she were seeing inside him. Inside to the lies and deception.

"All right. I'll agree to that," she said quietly. "Just let me get my purse."

She left him standing by the table and for one split

second as she disappeared through the doorway, Jack
thought about leaving. He didn't want to take her
money. And he damn well didn't want to keep digging
himself deeper and deeper into her life.

But what good would it do for him to leave? he argued with himself. She would only follow him. She felt
as if she owed him now, and it was obvious the last
thing she wanted to be was in his debt. The idea stung
him like an angry yellow jacket.

Jamming his hands into the pockets of his jeans, he
walked over to the door leading out to the patio.
Through the window he could see the shadows length-
ening across the backyard. Soon it would be dark and
the moonvine twined around the arbor would burst into
bloom with big white blossoms. Jack couldn't remember if his home in Houston had any blooming flowers
or shrubs. Irene wrote a gardener a check each month
to make sure the grounds were kept up, but Jack hardly
noticed as he headed to and from work. In fact, he rarely
ever went out in the yard for any reason. He was too
busy working. But he liked Grace's yard and cozy patio,
the color, and the scents of the blossoms.

The sound of her returning footsteps broke into his
thoughts and he turned to see her walking toward him.
As his gaze swept furtively up and down the length of
her, it dawned on him that the rounded shape of her
stomach was, in its own way, as beautiful as her face.

"Here's two fives," she said, extending the bills out
to him.

Jack had rather let a snake bite him on the hand than
take her money. He'd be blind to not see how desperately she needed it. But he didn't want to risk another
flood of tears by arguing anymore. Somehow he'd find
a way to give the money back to her.

"Thank you, Grace," he murmured, then unable to stand it any longer, he muttered an oath and reached for her shoulders. Quickly, his hands slid downward and spread against the small of her back.

Confusion widened her eyes and he wondered if she ____ the anguished longing he was feeling at this

"Jack, w___"

"Taking your money is stupid, Grace. Just about as stupid as this—"

As he lowered his head toward hers, he glimpsed her brows pulling together in puzzlement. Surprise parted her lips just before his settled down over them. The intimate contact created a moan deep in her throat and the needy sound urged Jack on. He pulled her closer until her breasts and belly were pressed tight against his bare chest. His tongue thrust past her sharp white teeth at the same time his fingers delved into the thick fall of hair at her back.

In all his life he could never remember tasting anything ___ this woman in his arms. She was like sipping war___ ___dy on a cold, cold night. Heat infused his body ___ he could feel himself burgeoning with the need to ___ inside her.

Soft, s___der arms curled around his neck and then her fingers ___re in his hair, the pads sliding against his scalp beggi___ ___m not to lift his head and end the kiss.

Jack's han___ moved from her back to her front as they first slid over her stomach, then up to the full ripe breasts pushing against the jersey fabric of her blouse. He desperately wanted to touch and taste her soft skin, to see her womanly curves unveiled. He wanted to hold her breasts in his palms and kiss the nipples. The same nipples her baby would suckle.

If only the life growing inside her had been put there by him. Oh, how he wished it.

The thought was so shattering, so totally unexpected, it frightened the hell out of Jack. Before he realized what he was doing, he jerked himself away from her and headed toward the door.

"Jack, what— Are you leaving?"

Her hoarse, tortured voice forced him to glance back at her. The wounded look on her face made him sick with guilt and self-recrimination.

"Don't you think it's about time?"

She walked toward him and Jack forced himself to stand his ground. But he knew if she touched him, he'd be lost to her. He was scared to death that he already might be.

"Yes, I guess it is," she whispered miserably. "Now do you understand why I was so upset before? I wanted to keep things between us—well, I don't want you getting close to me in any way. I can't let you, Jack. I've got to think about the baby and myself."

Everything she was saying was right and sensible. Yet Jack hated every word. "A few moments ago your kiss was telling me you couldn't get close enough."

Color flooded her cheeks and regret marred her features. Glancing away from him, she said, "I am human. And sometimes a woman needs to feel wanted. Don't spoil it all now and tell me you didn't want me. At least for a minute or two."

"I'm not that good of a liar, Grace."

Then before she could stop him, he was out the door. And she was left trembling, wondering desperately why she wanted to run after him.

Chapter Seven

It was late that night before Jack had collected himself enough to call his sister back in Houston. And even then, he punched in the numbers reluctantly. But then everything he'd done here lately was done with reluctance, he thought grimly.

Earlier this evening after he'd left Grace's, he'd gotten into his car and driven to Gulfport, then turned around and driven the thirteen miles back to Biloxi for no other reason than to force himself to concentrate on the traffic and the scenery around him rather than the aching need he felt for Grace.

Out of desperation, he stopped by the Lady Luck and played a few hands of blackjack. He'd taken Grace's two fives and turned them into more than a hundred. He wondered what the hell she was going to say about that when he turned the money over to her.

"Hello? Hello? Is anyone there?"

Suddenly he realized Jillian's voice was shouting in his ear.

"Hi, sis. Were you in bed?"

"Jack! What are you doing?" she gasped with surprise. "Is anything wrong?"

Naturally she would think something was wrong. He rarely ever called his sister. He always depended on her to keep the two of them in touch.

"Nothing is wrong. I just thought I'd call and see how you're doing."

She began to cough in earnest and Jack rolled his eyes. "Oh, come on, sis, I'm not that bad about calling, am I?"

"Not really. I guess the average of one call a year is better than nothing. So what's the matter? Been working late and decided you needed a break?"

He stretched his legs out in front of him as he carefully measured his next words. "No. Actually, I'm not working and haven't been for the past few days. I'm down in Biloxi. Taking a little vacation."

There was a long pause on the line, then she asked, "Jack, are you drunk?"

He forced himself to chuckle. Above anything else, he didn't want to give Jillian the suspicion that anything was amiss.

"I haven't been drunk in years. I just decided I needed a few days off, and Irene assured me she could hold down the fort."

"Nobody but Irene could hold it down. And I'm glad you've finally decided you need a break, Jack. Maybe while you're down there you'll learn there's more to life than winning a case."

Avoiding a case, namely one at your son, is what I'm trying to deal with, Jack wanted to say. Instead he said, "I'm not trying to do that much deep thinking, sis. Just using the time away from the office to enjoy the sand and water and a few beers. And the solitude.''

"Oh, so you're down there alone? I expected you to have a girlfriend with you.''

"Your brother has sworn off women.''

She laughed. "Since when?''

Since he'd met a goddess with black hair, green eyes and berry-red lips. "As soon as I realized they were making me miserable.''

She clucked her tongue in disapproval. "Jack, I do wish you didn't have such a bitter indifference toward women. We aren't all bad.''

"Not you, sweet sister.''

"Oh, my, you must be wanting something in exchange for that remark.''

Men always expect something in return for even the smallest favor. Their actions always have their own self-interest at heart.

It appeared as though Grace was right about men. Even him, he thought guiltily.

"No. I just wanted to hear your voice tonight…to remind myself I did still have family.''

"Jack,'' she said with great affection, "you know I always carry you around in my heart. All we've ever really had in this world is each other.''

"You have Trent,'' he pointed out.

"Yes. At least I was blessed before Paul decided he didn't want a wife and kid hindering his playboy lifestyle.''

Jack rubbed a palm over the stubble on his jaws and chin as he tried to decide just how much he could ask about his nephew without Jillian suspecting anything.

"By the way, how is my nephew?''

"He's great. He got the job he was wanting so badly. The one with American Oil."

"In Houston?"

"Yes. Isn't it wonderful?"

A part of Jack wasn't so sure it was wonderful. Why should Trent be so blessed while Grace was here suffering and trying her best to manage alone? The idea sickened him.

"Good for him. Making a great salary, I suppose?"

She named an impressive figure, then laughed. "And from the looks of things, he's going to need it. He's been getting pretty serious about a young woman here in Houston."

Grimacing, Jack rose to his feet and walked across the small space to a window that faced Grace's house. A light was burning in one of the rooms on this side and he couldn't help but wonder what she was doing and if she, like him, was still remembering their kiss.

"So you think your son has marriage on his mind?"

"I wouldn't be surprised if he didn't say they were engaged any day now. That's what I'm hoping for. She's a lovely girl from a nice, respected family. And I can hardly wait to have a grandchild."

Jack closed his eyes and pinched the bridge of his nose. He wasn't about to tell his sister that she already had a grandchild on the way. Even though Jillian had a big heart, she would be devastated that her son had shirked his responsibilities as a man and that Trent had apparently turned out to be no better than his own ne'r-do-well father. It wasn't the way Jillian would want a grandchild. And knowing what little he did about Grace, she wouldn't want her baby to have a grandmother simply out of a sense of duty.

"So she's from a nice, respected family in Houston,"

he repeated dryly. "That's so important to you, isn't it?"

"Jack! That's an awful thing to say! You know I'm not a snob!"

"Oh, come off it, Jillian, you know you wouldn't be nearly as happy if Trent brought in some poor girl who'd never heard of a debutante ball much less being turned out at one."

"Well, no, I have to admit I wouldn't be…but not for the reasons you're thinking," she said in a hurt voice. "I have enough common sense to know if Trent married a poor girl it would never last."

It probably wouldn't last with a rich one, either, Jack wanted to say. He heaved out a heavy breath then wiped a hand over his face. "I'm sorry, Jillian. I shouldn't have said that to you."

"You've gotten so cynical, Jack, it sometimes frightens me."

"I didn't mean to hurt your feelings, sis." But all the while she'd been gloating over Trent's oncoming engagement, all he could think about was Grace. Her kindness, her gentleness, her pride. She was as good or better than any socialite princess who'd been brought up on her daddy's wealthy knee. But as far as Jack was concerned, Jillian would never know about Grace and her connection to Trent. "You'll just have to overlook me. I'm…going through some things right now…that, well, are hard to deal with."

"Jack," his sister said with gentle concern, "we both know you need to leave the firm, so I'm not going to bother lecturing you about that. All I'm going to say is that you need to make a change in your life. A drastic change. Or you're never going to be happy."

He sighed. "Coming to Biloxi is a start. Give me

credit for that. And maybe before long I will make some sort of decision about the firm.''

"I wish you would also decide you wanted a wife and family.''

Jack laughed mockingly. "Start over at my age? You're crazy, sis."

"You're a young man, Jack. You need a wife and children. All these years you've been trying to fill that void inside you with work. It's not the same, believe me.''

Jack grimaced. He didn't need this from Jillian. She never lectured him and why she'd chosen tonight to do it made him wonder if that higher being in heaven thought he needed to be tested or even tortured for some reason.

"I don't see you making an effort to get married. And you've been single a helluva lot longer than I have.''

There was another long pause, then Jillian said, "Believe me, Jack, if I could find the right person I wouldn't hesitate. But love is something special. You don't find it on just any tree. Some people never find it. I hope to God if you ever do, you won't mess around and lose it.''

Jack wanted to tell her there was no such thing as love. Not anymore. The courtrooms were already full of divorce cases. Marriages ended everyday. Two kids and plenty of money hadn't been able to keep his parents as husband and wife. And nothing could have held him and Lenore together. No, Jack didn't need any more of that. He'd tried the thing called love and in the process he'd learned it didn't exist.

"Jack! Did you here me? Are you still there?''

Shaking away his thoughts, he turned from the window. "Sorry, sis, what were you saying?''

"I was asking if you're staying in your beach house. The one you let Trent borrow back in the winter."

If he'd had any lingering doubts that Trent had stayed here in the bungalow, his sister had just dissolved them.

"Yes, I am. Why?"

She chuckled. "I was just hoping he didn't leave things in a mess for you. He never was very good at cleaning up after himself."

Jack silently cursed. For a long time before Paul had divorced her, Jillian had deluded herself about the man. She'd only wanted to see the few good things in him and none of the bad. Obviously, she was doing the same with her son.

"I didn't find a mess," he assured her. At least not in the house, he thought grimly. Then before she could say more, he quickly ended the conversation with a promise to call her soon.

The next morning Jack was nailing down a loose shutter on the front of the bungalow when he spotted Grace walking down the driveway to her car. She was wearing a long pink dress splashed with tiny blue flowers. In one hand was a straw purse, the other, a white book resembling a bible.

It was Sunday. Grace was on her way to church.

Bolting off the stepladder, Jack intercepted her just as she was reaching for the handle on the car door.

"Good morning, Grace."

She turned to face him and he was instantly surprised to see a faint smile on her face. After that reckless encounter in her kitchen last night, he hadn't known what to expect from her.

"Good morning, Jack."

Her hair was fastened on both sides with pearl combs.

Pearl drop earrings dangled from her ears, while a strand circled her throat. The morning sun was kissing her skin, turning it to a golden rose. She looked lovely and rested, and just gazing at her filled Jack with warm contentment. "Going to church?"

She nodded, then glanced at the hammer in his hand. "Are you building something?"

"Just doing a little repair work on the house. I...had something to talk to you about. But it can wait," he said, thinking of the money he'd brought back from the Lady Luck.

"Would you like to come to church with me?" she invited.

His brows lifted, then he laughed. "Me in church? Grace, the roof might fall in."

Smiling, she shook her head. "I doubt it. We're all sinners."

Yes, and these past few days he'd become an even bigger one, he thought. But that was going to change. Last night after he'd talked with Jillian, he was convinced that Trent had used Grace, then went back to his life of luxury without any remorse or second thought. Jack didn't want his sister hurt by his son's low behavior. But the more he was beginning to know Grace, the more certain he was that she would never sue for a part of Trent's fortune. Now the main thing troubling Jack was how to tell Grace he'd been lying to her.

"I'm not dressed for church," he reasoned.

"Your khakis and shirt are fine. We're not a dressy, affluent congregation," she said with a reassuring smile.

"All right," he agreed. "Let me put my tools up and then I'll drive us. And afterwards, I have something I want you to help me with."

* * *

Not since her grandfather's passing had Grace had someone of her own to sit beside her in church. All through the sermon as she sat close to Jack's side, sharing her bible with him, his presence filled her with a sense of warmth and well being.

Each time she turned her head and met his gaze, he smiled at her. A faint, gentle smile that made Grace believe he was glad to be there with her.

After the service was over several of Grace's friends and acquaintances approached the two of them. As she introduced them to Jack, she was vaguely surprised and happy to see him shake hands and greet each one with complete sincerity. His attitude was quite a switch from the hard cynicism he'd shown her when he'd first arrived in Biloxi a few days ago. It made her wonder if she was the only person privy to that side of him, or if these past few days here in Mississippi were beginning to soften him.

"Thank you for coming to church with me, Jack," she said as they climbed into his sleek sedan to leave the church parking lot. "It was nice having you with me."

He glanced at her as he twisted the key in the ignition. "Thank you for inviting me, Grace. You have a nice church. It's the first one ever that I've felt comfortable in. I got the feeling everyone was there to worship, not just to see what the other person was wearing."

She laughed softly. "I told you none of the members were rich. They're just simple folk. By the way, you didn't have to put that large bill in the offering plate."

He glanced at her sharply. "I wasn't aware you saw that."

Grace had noticed he'd carefully folded the bill so that no one would see it or suspect that he'd been the one to place it in the offering tray. The fact that he'd not done it to impress had given Grace a new respect for the man.

"It was a generous gesture."

Her praise made him more than uncomfortable, especially when he was beginning to feel more and more like the biggest fraud that ever walked the earth.

"Are you free for the afternoon?" he asked.

She turned her head to look at him. The expression on his profile was smooth, telling her nothing of what was going on in his head.

"Yes. Why?"

"I thought you might go with me to the supermarket. I need to shop for groceries. You can consider it a job, if it makes you feel better."

Grace knew she ought not to be going anywhere with the man. But he'd gone to church with her without any protest and been very gracious to her friends. She could hardly refuse him now.

"All right," she agreed, then cast him a furtive, sidelong glance. "Does this mean you're going to be staying longer than you first planned?"

He didn't answer immediately and Grace found she was holding her breath in anticipation.

"I'm not sure...how long I'll be staying."

"What does that mean?"

He flashed her an irritated look. "It means I haven't made up my mind yet. Why? Already tired of having a neighbor."

She folded her hands atop her stomach and stared out the passenger window. "I made a mistake by trusting my last neighbor."

If Jack was smart he'd use this moment to come

clean, to tell her who he was and explain why he'd kept his connection to Trent a secret, or at least try to reason it out to her. But deep inside him, he knew the truth was going to make Grace hate him and he wasn't quite ready to give up this time with her. She made him feel young and fresh. She almost made him believe he could start over again.

"I have no intentions of hurting you, Grace."

Her gaze still on the passing street, she said, "Maybe you don't, but we seem to…rub each other the wrong way…at the wrong time."

"Look, Grace, last night—"

"I'm still confused over last night, Jack. And I don't really want to talk about it now."

He flipped on the turn signal and headed the sedan into a supermarket parking lot.

"Why? Because it embarrasses you? Because now that you've had time to think about it you don't want to admit you enjoyed kissing an old man like me?"

She turned an incredulous look on him. "Are you out of your mind? As far as I'm concerned, your age doesn't enter into anything about last night. And I'll remind you again, you're not old."

He let out a heavy breath as he parked the car in a slot not too far from the front entrance of the store. "If my age has nothing to do with it, then—"

Her green eyes were suddenly pleading as they scanned his face. "Can't you understand, Jack? It frightens me to death to think about trusting another man. I realize I kissed you in a way that contradicts that. But I'll admit I'm attracted to you. Very, very attracted. Still, that doesn't make it right or sensible."

Jack leaned over in the seat and gently framed the side of her face with his hand. "Since I've met you,

Grace, I seem to continue to make a fool of myself. I don't normally behave like this.''

Grace couldn't help it. The touch of his hand melted her heart. "So how do you behave with other women?"

One corner of his mouth curled upward in a sheepish grin. "Not nearly this nice."

Suddenly she was laughing and Jack was relieved. He hadn't meant for their conversation to get so serious. He hadn't really meant to bring up that heated kiss they'd shared last night. But when he was with Grace, he lost control of himself. Something he'd never allowed himself to do in the past.

"Come on," he urged, "let's get the shopping done. I'm getting hungry."

Inside the grocery store, Grace walked alongside him down the produce aisle. "Just what am I supposed to be doing for you, Jack? Telling you what items you need for cooking meals?"

He shook his head. "I want you to start putting anything and everything in this cart that you like or think you might want to eat."

She laughed. "We're shopping for you. Not me. You start picking out what you like and I'll show you how to choose fruit and vegetables and the best brands."

"No, Grace. These are going to be your groceries. Well, I might eat part of them," he conceded, "but the majority will be yours."

She stopped in her tracks, forcing Jack to halt the cart beside a bin of watermelons.

"Jack, please let's not argue in here," she said in a hushed voice. "The other customers will hear us. It'll be embarrassing."

He gave her a smug smile. "Then don't argue."

"I won't let you pay for my groceries. It isn't your place."

"I'm not paying for them, Lady Luck is."

She shot him a puzzled look. "What are you talking about?"

"I took the two fives you gave me for working on your air conditioner and played them at the blackjack table. You have lucky money, Grace. It doubled itself several times over."

She opened her mouth, then snapped it shut. "You're unbelievable, Jack. Sometimes I wonder if I should believe anything you tell me."

Jack wished he could swear that everything he'd ever said to her was the truth, but he couldn't. And it made him realize just how much he needed and wanted Grace's trust.

"If you don't believe me, you can ask the dealer. He'll remember the hefty tip I gave him."

"Ha! Just like I'm supposed to believe it was my two fives you used and not your own money."

He let out a frustrated breath. "I had already anticipated this argument from you. That's why I didn't just offer you the money. I knew you wouldn't accept it. So I decided you could use groceries to cook for the both of us."

Grace wasn't so sure she should be cooking any more meals for the two of them to eat together. Sharing a meal with Jack felt too much like a family thing and she couldn't let herself think of the two of them in that way. But she had agreed to cook for him, she reminded herself. She would be breaking her word if she reneged on the deal now. And she didn't want to come across as that kind of person. Especially when Jack was being so generous.

But why *is* he being so generous? Grace asked herself. Was she crazy to think he might simply want to help her because she needed it? Or would he prove to be a typical man and eventually want something from her in return?

Don't be stupid, Grace scolded herself. What could Jack possibly want from her? She was eight months pregnant and resembled a walrus. He wouldn't want sexual favors from her. And other than that, there was nothing else a woman like her had to give. Except her heart, and she was smart enough to know Jack didn't want her love.

No, she continued to ponder, he had to be offering her this help and attention just because he wanted to. The same way he'd given to the church.

Suddenly feeling much better about it all, she smiled at him. "All right. Let's get busy. I'm dying for lunch. We'll get something fast for it. Maybe something out of the deli," she added with growing excitement. "You'll let me do the choosing?"

He chuckled. It was amazing how much the happiness on her face affected him. How good it made him feel. He'd never imagined the mere smile on a person's face could do so much to him.

"Of course," he told her. "We could even carry it down to the beach and have a picnic if you want."

She looked at him with wide, uncertain eyes. "You really want to?"

He shrugged while wondering for the umpteenth time what was coming over him. He'd not done anything so frivolous since he was fifteen years old. He wasn't even sure he'd done it then. "Sure. It's Sunday. You don't plan on working today, do you?"

"No. What were you planning?"

He done so little work in the past few days it was indecent. He'd planned to write more notes on the pharmaceutical trial, but here he was with Grace instead.

"To work."

She cast him an empathetic smile. "You poor thing. It sounds like you've forgotten how to have a little fun on the beach."

Jack wasn't so sure he'd ever known how to have fun. All of his adult life he'd spent working. At least, that was all he remembered about it. As for his childhood, that period had not been a particularly happy time for him. If he hadn't been at boarding school, he'd been listening to his mother's spoiled tantrums or waiting for the rare occasion when his father would be home from the office. Fun had not been a plentiful commodity in the Barrett house.

His expression turned rueful. "I'm not exactly a fun kind of guy, Grace. Think you can show me how?"

"I'll try," she promised, then quickly caught him by the arm. "Wait, Jack, you've passed the watermelons. And we need one of those for dessert."

Jack never ate watermelon. He never went to the grocery store. And he never picnicked on the beach. But at this very moment he felt more alive than he had in a long, long time.

Chapter Eight

An hour of shopping was enough to fill the trunk of Jack's car. Once they got back to Grace's house, he carried in sack after sack, while Grace put the items away.

"My refrigerator and cupboards are bulging at the seams. They've never seen this much food before," Grace exclaimed as she finished with the last sack. "This will be enough to last until the baby gets here."

Surprise flickered across his face. "You mean, the baby will be here that soon?"

"Four weeks. Give or take a little. The doctor says the delivery date is difficult to pinpoint with the first one."

In a month, maybe less, Grace would be a mother. To his nephew's baby. There was Barrett blood flowing through the baby's veins. The fact filled Jack with an odd mixture of emotions that he couldn't begin to understand. All Jack knew for certain was that he wanted this woman and child to be cared for. Not just for now, but also into the future. And how he planned to get that accomplished was something Jack hadn't yet figured out.

"Do you know the sex?"

Smiling briefly, she shook her head. "Before the ultra-sound, I told the doctor I didn't want to know. Life meant for us to have surprises. Don't you think?"

Jack had always hated surprises. Especially in the courtroom. He was a man who liked knowing every angle, every possibility beforehand. A person could stay in control that way. The philosophy had made him a hell of a good lawyer. But as for the sort of man it had made of him, he couldn't say. These past few days he was beginning to get the idea he'd been missing out on far more than he could ever imagine.

"I suppose," he said offhandedly, then gestured toward the picnic basket on the table. "Are you finished packing our lunch?"

She shook her head, then glanced down at her dress. "No. But almost. And I need to change my clothes. Do you plan to swim?"

"I hadn't thought about it."

"You'd better go change, too," she suggested. "You'll get hot in trousers. And you sure can't swim in them."

"You're right," he agreed. "I'll meet you back here in a few minutes."

Grace finished packing the rest of the food into the large cane basket, then hurried to the bedroom to change out of her dress. She'd outgrown her swimsuit several months ago, so she slipped on the shortest pair of shorts she could find and a loose tank top that was dark enough not to be see-through once it was wet.

After securing her hair into a ponytail, she carried the

basket of food onto the front porch. At the same time
Jack was climbing the steps to meet her.

His long, muscled legs were exposed by navy swimming trunks while a gray-and-navy cotton shirt had
been left unbuttoned to flap loosely against his bare
chest. He looked like a bronzed lion, Grace thought. All
muscle and power and a fierceness that could be un-
leashed in less than a heartbeat.

"Here, I'll take that," he told her.

She gratefully handed him the basket. "Are we going
to walk down to this beach or did you want to drive
somewhere else?"

He made an open gesture with his hand. "You're the
one who knows the best beaches around here."

She smiled, then feeling suddenly brave and light-
hearted she looped her arm through his. "Then we'll
walk. We have the best beach right here in front of us.
And it's usually very private."

Not far from the surf's edge, beneath the shade of a
pine, Grace spread a blanket, then took a seat on one
end. Jack placed the picnic basket in front of her, then
sat cross-legged a few inches away from Grace and
watched her spread out the items she'd purchased at the
supermarket deli.

There were cold sodas, fried chicken, cole slaw, po-
tato salad, and baked beans. To that she'd added pick-
les, olives, cheeses and fruit, including a hefty slice of
the watermelon.

"This is enough food for a whole party of people,"
Jack teased. "Did you forget there's only two of us."

She laughed. "I'm eating for two and I stay ravenous.
Everything looks good when you're hungry." She
handed him a paper plate and utensils. "Dig in," she
invited.

They both filled their plates and began to eat. After a couple of minutes, Jack said with mild surprise, "I never much liked deli food. But this is delicious."

Grace smiled knowingly. "Everything tastes better when you eat it out of doors. And especially on the beach."

He looked thoughtfully off toward the gently rolling surf. "On most days back in Houston, I couldn't tell you what I eat. My secretary calls out for something and puts it in front of me. I'm usually forced to gobble it down between phone calls. I never stop to think about the taste, I'm just more or less refueling my body."

She scowled at him. "That's terrible, Jack. Food is meant to be savored and celebrated. It's no wonder your doctor ordered you out of the office. What about when you're at home? Don't you take time for a leisurely meal then?"

He grimaced. "I always get home at a late hour, by then the housekeeper, who also cooks for me, has gone home. So I heat up whatever she's made and eat it while I read briefs or depositions."

Grace clucked her tongue with disapproval. "There's times I get loaded with class work, but I never do that. Elias used to say, your work will still be here when you're old and dead and gone. And then none of it will matter, so you'd better take time to enjoy the roses while you're here."

He glanced at her and was instantly mesmerized by the open affection on her face. Obviously she had loved her grandfather very much and Jack could understand why. From what she'd told him so far, the old man had been the only solid rock in her life.

"What did your grandfather do? For a living, I mean?"

"From the time he was a boy until he got too old, he was a shrimper. He enjoyed being on the water, almost as much as he did playing the fiddle. That's where I acquired my love of music."

"Did he teach you how to play?"

She nodded fondly, then laughed. "He played totally by ear and that's how I learned, too, so when I started taking regular lessons, the teacher had an awful time making me read music. I thought it was such a waste."

"So you also play by sheet music now?"

She laughed again. "Oh, yes. I couldn't be a teacher without knowing all the theory." Her smiling eyes settled on his face. "I wish you could have known Elias. He could fiddle Cajun music as good or better than the best of them. No matter how tired you might be, when he picked up his bow and pulled it across the strings, you just had to get up and dance."

Grinning, Jack shook his head. "Not me. I have two left feet when it comes to dancing."

Grace clucked her tongue again. "Jack, I'm beginning to worry more and more about you. You don't ever picnic or play on the beach. You don't take time to eat a pleasurable meal. You don't dance. I'm afraid to ask what you do for enjoyment."

He shrugged as he gnawed off a bite of drumstick. "You sound like my doctor. He says I need to be doing anything but working."

"Sounds like he's a smart doctor. You should take his advice."

"I am. For today at least."

As Grace chewed her food, she swept a furtive glance over his tanned features. She had to admit he didn't appear quite as fatigued as when he'd first come to Biloxi, but there was still a strained look about him. As though, deep down, he never felt relaxed or at peace with himself.

Grace would have liked to know what was eating at him, but she very much doubted he shared that part of himself with anyone. He would probably resent it if she asked him to.

"Do you work so much because you need to, or because you just want to?" she asked.

He'd finished the food on his plate and now as he filled it with cheese and fruit, he thought how, earlier in the supermarket parking lot, he'd been wishing he could be totally honest with Grace. Maybe now was the time to start.

"As far as money goes, I could stop work now and never have to lift a hand. Along with what the firm brings in, I've made many investments down through the years that have proved to be very profitable. I don't need the money."

"Then you do it because you like it," Grace stated.

While he pondered her words, Grace watched the sea breeze play with his hair, tossing the loose waves here and there about his head. She'd not ever been particularly drawn to men with longer hair. In fact, most of the young men she'd been acquainted with in college had severely short haircuts. Yet there was something very sensual about Jack's tawny mane touching the back of his collar and at times, falling waywardly onto his forehead. It was as much a part of him as his steel-gray eyes and sardonic smile.

"Why the hell else would I be doing it if I didn't like it?"

She frowned at his sarcasm, but didn't let it put her off. "I don't know. Maybe you should tell me," she said.

For long moments he merely gazed out at the ocean, his expression vacant. Then, finally, he looked at her and said, "All right, Grace, I'll tell you. I keep doing it because I—giving it up would seem like failing to me. And I don't ever lose, Grace. Losing just isn't in me."

There was an anguished sort of resolution in his voice that tormented Grace. Leaning forward, she placed her hand on his forearm.

"Jack, it's okay for a person to lose once in a while. It doesn't mean you're a failure. You're an intelligent man, you ought to know that."

The warmth of her fingers combined with her gentle expression touched Jack much more than he wanted to admit. He couldn't remember any woman, other than his sister, who'd ever cared about his wants or needs. His mother, his ex-wife, his last girlfriend, and all the women in between were more interested in what his high-powered job could do for them, not what it meant to Jack himself.

With a rough sigh, he placed his empty plate to one side. "Logically, I do know that, Grace. But old habits die hard. Even when you know they're not necessarily good for you."

Turning toward her, he lifted her hand in his and studied the back of her smooth skin. She wore no rings and her nails were short and practical instead of long and glamorous, yet her hands were very sensual, he thought. Just looking at her slender brown fingers filled him with erotic images.

When she didn't make any sort of reply, he knew she expected him to explain. If it had been anybody else, he would have ended the discussion. Hell, he would have never started it in the first place. But Grace did something to him. He didn't want to disappoint her. In any way.

"You see, Grace," he went on, "my mother was...not a particularly loving person. My sister and I never wanted for material things, but we never really had a mother's love. Dad, on the other hand, showered us with love and attention. And I worshiped him for that. I wanted to please him in every way I could. I wanted him to be proud of me. Always."

"I'm sure he was," Grace said to him.

Jack nodded. "On the day I passed my bar exam, he was on top of the world. He predicted I would be a success and, thankfully, I didn't let him down. He went to his grave believing I would preserve the legacy he'd given me."

"Meaning the firm?"

He let out a heavy breath. "Yes."

Her fingers tightened perceptively around his. "Your father is gone now. You can feel good because you made him so happy while he was alive. But that part of your life with him is over. You should be concerned with making yourself happy now."

Put in Grace's simple terms it sounded right and reasonable. But the firm had been a wife to him down through the years, divorcing her would leave him with nothing.

"I'm happy enough. I'd be greedy to want more," he murmured. But he did want more than what he'd had so far, he thought. He wanted more than work. More than a woman who only cared about his wealth and position. He wanted someone like Grace.

But you can't have her, a mocking voice shouted silently back at him. She's going to have Trent's baby. She's going to hate you when she finds out you're his uncle. Besides, there's too many years between you. Your lives would never fit.

Desperate to end the plaguing thought, he tugged on her hand and urged her to her feet. "It's getting hot. Are you ready to go for a swim?"

Grace really wanted to move closer to him. She wanted to touch his face with her hand, kiss his lips and press her cheek against the strong column of his neck. She wanted to tell him that from this day forward he should start living for himself and allowing himself to be happy. But she could see he was through talking for the time being, so she simply nodded and allowed him to lead her down the beach to the water's edge.

Because the tide was low, they were forced to wade several yards before the water was deep enough to swim. Grace breast-stroked parallel to the coastline until she reached an old fishing pier made of wooden planks. By then she was out of breath, so she found her feet and from the shade of the pier watched Jack as he plowed further out to open water.

Several minutes passed before he swam to where she was standing. He was a bit winded, but she was still very much impressed and she smiled at him as he raked the wet hair back off his forehead.

"You must work out at the gym. You're in good shape."

He laughed at the idea. "According to my doctor I don't work out nearly enough. I used to play racquetball quite a bit. But now I do well to run on the treadmill every day."

"Between your visits to the courtroom and your office and your gobbled meals?" she asked, then shook her head. "Must be a hectic schedule."

"It is. That's why I've got to keep my heart in good condition. My old man died of a heart attack."

Tilting her head back, she looked into his face. At the moment his dark lashes were spiked. Beads of water clung to his cheeks and lips, making Grace wish she could lap them away with her tongue.

The notion lowered the timber of her voice as she asked, "Did you ever stop to think the heart needs more than just exercise to survive?"

He let out a mocking laugh, then before he could say more, a wave roared against them, pushing Grace straight at Jack. To keep from toppling over, she grabbed his wet shoulders. At the same time, she felt his hands slide to the back of her waist.

He took a moment to steady her on her feet. But instead of releasing her, he continued to hold her against him as he studied her wet face. "I'm beginning to believe you're old-fashioned, Grace," he murmured.

Her heart was suddenly pounding. "You're probably right. Oftentimes I believe I was born too late. I—I'm not like most of my young female friends. I relate better to older people."

One corner of his lip curled upward as his eyes kept up their lazy inspection of her face. "Why is that?"

Her gaze dropped to his chest. Drops of water clung to the bronze skin and curly hair growing thickly between his nipples. Being next to him like this, with the buoyancy of the warm water wrapping around them like soft velvet, was the most sensual thing Grace had ever experienced. She wanted to kiss him so badly she could hardly concentrate on his question.

"Because—I have different notions about life. I have more simple, antiquated ideas, I guess you'd say. About home and family and a woman's place in the world.

Maybe that comes from being mostly raised by my grandfather.''

His hand came beneath her chin to lift her face back up to his. "And maybe it comes from being a romantic," he suggested softly.

Her heart slowed, her eyes went solemn. "You're wrong about that, Jack. I'm not a romantic. Not after— well, not anymore."

He grimaced and then his hands slid to her stomach where his fingers worshiped the fullness pressing against him. Not until he'd spent this time with Grace had he ever stopped to think what a wondrous thing it was for a woman to give a man a child. And even though the baby inside her wasn't his, he still wanted to shelter and protect it, to think of it as his own. He knew he was being a fool. He knew the idea was reckless and crazy, yet he couldn't seem to stop himself.

"You're bitter because Trent hurt you," he said. "But deep down you're still the same woman who wants to be loved. Who wants a family of her own. Didn't you say that?"

Her green eyes were suddenly flooded with anguish. "I don't think I'll ever trust any man enough to—to want to have a family with him. I don't think I'll ever let myself get that close to a man again. Unless I was convinced he really loved me."

His hands pushed boldly upward until they were cupping both her breasts. Grace's fingers tightened on the muscles of his shoulders even as she told herself to back away from him.

"You're letting yourself get close to me," he whispered.

Color poured into her already rosy cheeks. "Yes. And for the life of me I don't know why I am. Or why you'd even want to get close to me," she argued. "I may be naive in lots of ways, Jack, but I'm not stupid. I realize you can have your pick of women. So I don't understand why you're wasting your time flirting with a fat, pregnant one."

Her black hair glistened in wet, shiny strands around her face. He thrust his fingers against her scalp, then slid them slowly through her hair until they were pressing against the back of her neck. She had no idea how lovely or desirable she was to him.

"Hell, yes, I can have my pick. It's easy for a rich man to get women. But just how much do you think I get out of that, when I know each one of them is looking at what I can buy her rather than at me."

She studied his face for long, weighty moments. "From all that you've told me, I would think you like things that way. Without strings or attachments of the heart."

Glancing away from her, he muttered a curse just under his breath. "I used to think it was exactly all that I wanted. But not anymore. Even the sex is meaningless to me now."

His admission caused her to gasp sharply. His lips curled sardonically at the sound. "Does that shock you, Grace?" He glanced back at her. "Well, this ought to shock you a lot more," he warned.

Before Grace could fathom his words, his head bent and his lips were on hers in a fiercely possessive kiss. At first she was too stunned to resist and then it was impossible to do anything except enjoy the rich, heady taste of his mouth against hers.

Only seconds passed before his tongue was thrusting past her teeth. She boldly met it with her own before she allowed him a deeper search of the intimate contours of her inner mouth. When he eventually found the tip of her tongue, then gently sucked, she groaned deep in her throat and pressed herself closer.

His hands dipped beneath the hem of her top then quickly found her breasts. Their centers were puckered into hard buds of excitement. He rubbed his thumbs across them, imagining the sweet milk she would give her child.

Barely lifting his head, he nipped her lips with his teeth, then grazed a hungry trail over her chin and down the tender line of her throat. Grace's hands slipped from his shoulders down to his chest where her palms flattened against his flat nipples, then gently rubbed up, then down. Around them the sluggish waves pushed them first one way and then the other, but never apart.

After a while Grace felt as if she was floating and then she realized her feet were no longer on the ocean floor. Her legs were wrapped around Jack's and he was holding the bulk of her weight against him.

She groaned out his name as his teeth sank into her soft earlobe. "Jack—we—you've got to stop," she pleaded between breathless pants.

He raised his head and looked at her with great concern. "Am I hurting you, Grace?"

The worry on his face made it even that much harder for Grace to resist him. "No. It's not that," she whispered miserably. "I—want you to make love to me, Jack. But I can't let you."

The lines of worry on his face deepened into a frown. "Why? Because it wouldn't be good for the baby?"

She shook her head and fought at the tears collecting in her throat. "No. Because it wouldn't be good for me."

Jack sucked in a deep breath in an effort to clear the

raw desire pumping through his veins. "Why?" he persisted.

Her hands framed his handsome face and for a moment it took every ounce of strength in her to keep from leaning forward and kissing his lips all over again. "You'll be gone from here soon, Jack. And once you're back in Houston, I'll be nothing to you but a dim memory. I've already let that happen to me once. I can't live through it again."

She didn't trust him. She thought he was another Trent. And she was right, he thought sickly. He wasn't prepared to offer her a lifetime commitment. And even if he was, he'd been lying to her. Maybe not in the same way Trent had lied, but still, the deception was there.

He released a long, heavy breath. "I'm sorry, Grace. You must be thinking I'm a real snake in the grass."

"No. But you probably have the idea that since I've already had one affair, and that I'm young and inexperienced, I'm an easy target for another one."

His hands tightened on her shoulders as he grimaced at her words. "I don't think any such thing. And I don't want to have an affair with you."

She looked away from him as heat flooded her face. "I see, you just had a one-time thing on your mind. Not anything as long-term as an affair."

He shook her slightly. "No, damn it. I didn't have any such thing on my mind. I—hell, I wasn't thinking at all. That's what you do to me, Grace."

Sighing, she bent her head and sank her teeth into her bottom lip. "That's what you do to me, too, Jack. We're—we seem to be bad for each other. Maybe...for the rest of your stay here in Biloxi we—shouldn't see each other." She suddenly lifted her face. "You can have your groceries back. I wouldn't keep them—not that way.''

He said, ''I don't give a damn about the groceries, Grace. It's you I want.''

She closed her eyes and prayed for willpower. ''Well, you can't have me.''

''Do you think I don't know that?'' he asked disgustedly.

''I don't know what to think or believe anymore,'' she whispered miserably.

His fingers tangled longingly in her silky hair. ''Would it make you feel better not to see me anymore?''

She shook her head, then opened her eyes to meet his troubled gaze. ''Maybe you'd be relieved if you weren't around me anymore.''

If Jack couldn't be with Grace, there would be no reason for him to stay here in Biloxi. And if he had to keep his distance from Grace, he wouldn't want to be anywhere. It was a staggering admission. And one that had him wondering when and how he'd let himself get into such a tangled web.

''No. I wouldn't like that, Grace. I enjoy your company. More than you'll ever know.''

Her green eyes softened and then, with a little broken sob, she flung her arms around his neck. ''Oh, Jack,'' she murmured against his cheek. ''You're the first person who's ever cared about me since—well, since my grandfather. I don't really want you to leave. You won't, will you?'' She leaned her head back and her eyes were beseeching as they scanned his face. ''I want you to be here when the baby comes. It would mean so much to me to have someone—to have you with me.

And then—well, I understand you'll have to go after that.''

Jack thought of the upcoming trials he had scheduled, of the many clients Irene had probably already diverted to his associates. One more week here in Biloxi was going to cost him dearly. Two more after that would put his rear in a vise. But for once he didn't care. He couldn't tell Grace no. And what was even more amazing, he didn't want to.

"I'll stay, Grace. Until the baby comes," he promised. "But right now I think I'd better get you back on the beach."

He lifted her into his arms and began to wade toward the shoreline. Grace tightened her hold around his neck and tried to hold back the joy filling her heart.

Everyone she'd ever cared about in her life had left her for one reason or another. Her dad and mother, her grandparents and Trent. But Jack was going to stay for a little while. He'd promised, and she believed him. She wasn't going to have to go through the trauma of having her baby alone. Someone finally cared enough to stay.

And afterwards when it did come time for him to go, how was she going to deal with that? she wondered. Well, she wasn't going to think about it this evening. Tomorrow would be soon enough to start worrying about a future without Jack.

Chapter Nine

By the next evening Jack was half crazy. He had to tell Grace the truth. There was nothing else left for him to do. She had to know he was Trent's uncle. But how, he wondered, was he going to tell her without making his intentions sound so...underhanded, so deliberately calculating?

Tossing the legal pad to one end of the cluttered desk, he stood and began to pace around the small bedroom.

There wasn't any way he could soften the truth, he thought miserably. He would simply have to admit that at first she'd been a stranger to him and his initial concern had naturally been for his nephew.

Naturally, he thought, mockingly. Family was supposed to be a man's first loyalty. If only he'd known Trent had grown up to be a spoiled mama's boy, then he would have never lied to Grace in the first place. He'd would have been more than happy to let Trent suffer whatever misery Grace wanted to deal him.

With a weary groan, he glanced back at the piled

desk. Last night after he and Grace had returned from the beach, he'd come home and tried to concentrate on his work. If he planned to stay here two or three more weeks, it was vital he fax back notes and necessary information for the pharmaceutical case. But in the end, he'd gotten very little work done and today he'd not faired much better.

As each hour ticked away he knew the time was dragging closer to when Grace would return from classes and the time for him to come clean would be upon him.

Face it, Jack, the only thing you can do now is break the news as gently as you can.

He stopped his pacing as his mind began to whirl with ideas. Maybe he could take her out to dinner. The truth might not sound so bad to her if she was told over candlelight. But both their kitchens were bulging with all the food they'd purchased yesterday at the market and Grace was a practical woman. She'd say they should eat what they have before wasting money on dining out. And anyway, it might be better if they were in a more private place when he told her. He didn't fancy being slapped in a busy restaurant.

Perhaps he could get a bottle of wine or champagne and invite her over here to share it with him, he considered. Then immediately cursed himself for such a stupid idea. Grace was pregnant. She couldn't drink alcohol of any kind. And a jug of milk just didn't have the same effect.

Jack glanced at his wristwatch. He figured he had two or three hours at the most before Grace got back home. By then he had to think of something. He'd uncovered some pretty awful truths in the courtroom and survived. This couldn't be any worse, he tried to assure himself. But it sure as hell felt like it would be.

* * *

Grace was tired when she got home from college classes that evening. But the fatigue was only physical. Her heart was no longer heavy. All day her spirit had sung a happy tune and she'd had trouble concentrating on the professor's lecture. She couldn't think about great composers when Jack was constantly lurking at the edge of her mind.

She could hardly wait to see him. To tell him about her day, to fix his dinner, to hear what he'd been doing. She needed the sound of his voice, the touch of his hand. Just being in his presence filled her with a warm glow and a sense of worthiness. For the first time in her life, Jack made her feel truly wanted. If all of that meant she was falling in love with the man, then she knew she was crazy. She knew she should put the brakes on her runaway heart. But how could she do that when Jack was filling up a hungry hole inside her?

After changing into a long white skirt splashed with big red roses and topping it with a loose red tank top, she walked over to the bungalow and tapped on Jack's door.

He opened it immediately and gestured for her to come in. "I'm glad you came over," he told her. "I was just about to call you."

"Oh? To tell me what you wanted me to cook for supper?"

A sheepish grin touched his face. "No. Actually, I'm cooking for you tonight."

She shot him a puzzled look and he motioned for her to take a seat on the couch.

After making herself comfortable, she said, "Look Jack, we've been all through this before. *I'm* the one who's supposed to be doing for you. Not the other way around."

He eased down beside her and took hold of her hand. "Don't argue with me this time, Grace. Tonight I— well, there's something I've been wanting to talk to you about."

She studied his grim expression and her heart was suddenly heavy with dread. Maybe she'd jumped the gun by putting her faith in Jack. Maybe he was going to leave after all, in spite of his promise.

"What is it?" she asked cautiously.

He shook his head. "I'll tell you in a few minutes. But first I wanted to give you something."

Her brows lifted as her fingers unconsciously fluttered to her bosom. "Give me?"

Standing, he reached behind the end of the couch. Grace was even more surprised to see him pull out a package all wrapped up with blue paper and a big white bow.

She chuckled as he handed the box to her. "What is this?" she asked teasingly. "A peace offering?"

He shot her a wary look. "We haven't been arguing."

She smiled broadly as she slipped a finger beneath the tape fastenings. "Not for the past twelve or fifteen hours. And anyway, I'm not one of those women who expect gifts. I really wished you hadn't done this, Jack."

He couldn't remember a time he'd ever felt like such a devious, two-faced heel. He rued the moment he'd first decided to keep his whole identity a secret from her.

"It's nothing frivolous, Grace. I didn't waste my hard-earned money," he tried to tease.

She shot him another smile and he decided she was in an exceptionally joyful mood tonight. She'd been that way ever since he'd told her he'd stay until the baby was born. He'd never imagined his promise would make her so happy and because it had, his heart was overflowing with a mixture of joy and apprehension.

"A gift for the baby!" she suddenly exclaimed as she pulled a tiny pair of denim overalls from a nest of tissue paper. "Oh, they're so adorable, Jack!"

"There's a cap to match, too," he told her.

She quickly dug back into the box, then squealed with delight as she held up the tiny baseball cap. "This is perfect! Thank you so much, Jack. And because it's a gift for the baby I won't fuss about the money you spent."

At least he'd earned one good mark for the evening. "How old will he have to be to wear those things?" Jack asked.

She held up the overalls as she tried to gauge the size and weight they were made to fit. "Oh, maybe four or five months old," she guessed, then shot him a sly look. "Wait a minute, did you say he?"

"It will be a boy," he said with certainty.

She laughed. "What makes you so sure? A little girl can wear overalls, too, you know."

"I know. But the baby will be a boy. With black hair and green eyes like yours." His mouth quirked with a faint smile. "And if he's lucky, he'll have your heart, too."

Touched by his words, she slipped her hand over his. "Jack," she said gently. "That's such a sweet thing for you to say."

He looked away from her and took in a deep breath. "I used to think a man didn't need much of a heart to get along in this world. But I'm beginning to think I might have been wrong. About a lot of things."

His gaze turned back to her and he knew this was the moment. He couldn't put it off any longer.

"Grace, I—"

He stopped as she suddenly looked toward the kitchen and sniffed. "Is that burning charcoal I smell?"

The grill. Jack had forgotten he's set a match to the stack of charcoal a few minutes before Grace had knocked on the door.

"Don't move," he ordered as he rose to his feet. "I'll be right back."

"I'll stay right here," she promised as he disappeared toward the kitchen.

Seconds later, she heard the back door slam and then her attention was drawn back to the overalls lying in the box. She picked them up and ran her fingers over the soft washed denim. This was the first gift her baby had received. Later, when she dressed him or her in it, she would always think of Jack.

The ring of the telephone suddenly ripped into her warm thoughts. Spotting the telephone on the end table next to her, her first inclination was to ignore it and simply tell Jack someone had called when he came back in. But it could be something pertaining to his work. Something important that he needed to know right away, she thought, and it wouldn't be any trouble to take a message.

She picked up the receiver. "Hello? Jack Barrett's residence," she answered.

"Hello? Is Jack there?" a female voice asked.

"Yes. But at the moment he's outside. Can I take a message? I'm his—housekeeper," she said for want of a better word.

The female on the other end chuckled with humor. "I should have known Jack wouldn't clean up after himself no matter where he was," she said, then added, "just tell him his sister called to give him the happy news that his nephew has gotten engaged."

"Okay. Will he know which nephew?"

"Trent is the only nephew he has. So he'll know."

Trent! Was she talking about the same Trent?

Grace's mind was so frozen with shock, she barely heard the woman's goodbye or the click of the receiver in her ear.

Numbly, she placed the phone back in its resting place, then glanced unseeingly around the room. It couldn't be true! Jack wouldn't keep something like that from her! All this time she'd been talking about Trent, how he'd forsaken her and the baby! If he was Trent's uncle, how could he have not have said something?

This had to be a mix-up. Some strange coincidence with names, she tried to assure herself. But Trent was from Houston. The same as Jack. He'd told her his family was rich and that his grandfather had been a well-known lawyer, but he'd never mentioned the Barrett name. Grace had naturally assumed it was Jurgenson, the same as Trent's. Now she knew Trent's rich grandfather had been a Barrett, and Jack's father.

The sound of Jack's returning footsteps brought her head around. When he stepped through the door, she was certain her heart was going to break right down the middle.

"Grace! What's wrong? You're as white as a ghost!"

"I have a message for you," she said flatly. "From your sister."

She didn't have to say more. The sick, wounded look on her face told him she knew.

His heart thudding heavily in his chest, Jack slowly went to the couch and took a seat close by her side.

Yet, when he reached for her hand, she quickly snatched it back.

"Grace," he began quietly, "this is what I wanted to talk to you about. When—"

"It's a little late, don't you think?" she interrupted coldly.

He shook his head with frustration. "Yes. I'll admit it's late. But I had my reasons for not telling you."

"I'm sure," she quipped, then rose to her feet. "But there's no need wasting my time or yours with explanations. As far as I'm concerned there's nothing else I want to hear from you."

She started to walk away, but Jack instantly grabbed her by the hand and pulled her back down beside him. "I deserve at least five minutes, Grace. Give me that, at least."

Her green eyes were blazing as they rapidly scanned his face. "You don't deserve anything! You're—no better than your sorry, lying nephew!"

Her words bit at him like the lash of a whip. "Grace, believe me, when I first came down here to Biloxi, I didn't know you even existed. I wasn't even aware that Trent had stayed here in my bungalow."

Her mouth popped open with further outrage. "You mean, this has always been your bungalow? You didn't just buy it?"

He shook his head. "It's been mine for two years or more. If Trent told you it was his, he was lying."

Her head wagged back and forth as she tried to digest all that he'd been saying. "Trent said it belonged to him. He said his family was rich and he'd bought the place just to have a beachside getaway."

"The little bastard!" Jack muttered.

She stabbed him with another glare. "If that's the

way you feel, why didn't you tell me you were his uncle right from the start?''

He sucked in a bracing breath, then slowly released it. "When you walked in here that first night, I didn't know what to think or believe. I had no idea what sort of connection, if any, you had to Trent. And then I began to worry about my sister. I thought if Trent really had gotten you pregnant, then you were bound to eventually sue for child support. Jillian has been through a lot of sorrow of her own. I didn't want her to go through more.''

"And lying to me was going to prevent that?" she asked with disbelief.

He shook his head with remorse. "I didn't think of it as lying. I was just avoiding the truth. I wanted to find out your intentions. If it turned out that you were planning to somehow gain access to the Barrett fortune, then I—well, I wasn't going to let you do that," he finished miserably.

"Oh, God," she whispered painfully. "You thought—you actually believed I would be capable of such a thing? How could you, Jack? How could you think that and then touch me as if—you really wanted me?" She shivered with revulsion. "After Trent left, I told myself I'd been conned by the perfect liar. But I'd been wrong. You have Trent beat by a mile!''

"I did really want you, Grace. I do! That has nothing to do with me being Trent's uncle," he tried to reason as his frustration turned to anger. Never had anyone's opinion of him mattered as much as Grace's. To know she now considered him lower than pond scum, cut Jack to the core. "And don't compare me to Trent! I haven't taken advantage of you!''

Her mouth fell open. "Then what have you been doing?"

"Damn it, Grace, don't you understand? I didn't know you at first. For all I knew, you could have been trying to snare a rich husband by trapping him with a baby. I was only trying to look out for the interest of my family."

"By lying to me," she said between gritted teeth. "You thought I was a gold digger. A slut of the worse kind. Well, I can't begin to tell you what I think you are! And a 'good' lawyer definitely isn't the word I have in mind!"

She tried to jerk her hand from his, but he purposely tightened his hold. "Grace, please listen. I admit I was very wrong. And it didn't take me long to see not only with my eyes, but also with my heart that you weren't a gold digger. But by then, I—well, I was afraid to tell you the truth, because I feared you were going to react like this and—I didn't want our time together to be ruined."

Grace was forced to turn her head away from him and swallow hard as tears scalded her throat. All the time he'd spent with her, all the nice things he'd done for her, had been done with subterfuge. His motive hadn't been kindness or concern or attraction. He'd simply been spying on her. Playing underground suitor with her heart. And she'd let herself believe he cared, that he really wanted to be with her. What a stupid fool she'd been.

"Well, it is ruined, Jack," she said in a choked voice. "I want you out of my life. And as far as your family and their money goes, I don't want anything to do with it or them! Now or ever! And I certainly don't want anything to do with you!"

"The baby—"

Her head jerked around to his as her free hand settled protectively over her stomach. "The baby is mine!" she said fiercely. "I don't care if you are a big-shot lawyer. I won't let you take it away from me!"

He stared at her with angry disbelief. "How could you think I would do such a thing to you, Grace?"

For a moment something on his face grabbed her heart and she was suddenly remembering the heat of his kiss, the rough warmth of his hands on her breasts. He'd made her feel things she'd never felt before. She'd wanted to give him every part of her, even her heart, she thought sadly.

"Because I just discovered I don't know you, Jack. You're not the man who went to church with me, who kissed me beneath the pier, who…promised to stay with me until the baby was born."

"I will stay."

Tears blurred her eyes as she jerked her hand from his and rose to her feet. "I never want to see you again. For any reason. I hope you go back to Houston…and bury yourself in that law office of yours. You deserve it!"

She headed toward the door and though Jack desperately wanted to stop her, he realized it would be useless to try to reason with her tonight.

As her hand twisted the knob, he said, "I'm sorry, Grace. I never meant to hurt you."

She paused to look back at him and Jack hated himself as he caught sight of a tear glistening on her cheek.

"No. You were just looking out for your family. And to hell with Grace Holliday. I understand completely, Jack."

He opened his mouth to deny her words, but she

stepped out the door, then slammed it behind her, cutting off any chance for him to say more. Jack wondered if this was how a felon felt when the cell door closed behind him and he knew his chance for a happy life was clearly over.

The next evening Jack's bags were packed and sitting by the door. The car was full of gas. All he had to do was carry everything out to the trunk and lock the house.

But so far he couldn't bring himself to make the final move. All day he'd been telling himself it was better this way. If he stayed around Grace much longer, he was going to do something really stupid like fall in love with her. And that would never work.

What was he thinking? he growled at himself. He couldn't fall in love with Grace. He didn't even believe the emotion existed.

Still, something had held him here all throughout the afternoon. The idea of driving off and never seeing Grace again filled him with agony. He wasn't ready to give her up.

Wake up, Jack. You never had Grace. Your time with her was doomed from the very start.

Ignoring the voice in his head, he snatched up the box on the end of the couch and headed out the door. Something was wrong. He'd seen Grace pull up in the driveway several hours ago. Since then, not one of her little violin students had shown up for their Tuesday evening lesson.

He didn't care how furious she was with him, he wanted the baby to have the overalls she left behind last night. And he had to find out what was going on with her.

After knocking several times on the front door and not getting any sort of answer, Jack called to her.

"Grace, I know you're in there. I'm not going to go away until I talk to you."

As long seconds ticked by, Jack began to grow uneasy. Grace wasn't one to run and hide. Even angry, she wouldn't ignore him. She would take pleasure in telling him to get off her porch.

With that thought in mind, Jack stepped into the house and went to find her. Moments later, he was stunned to find her in bed.

"Grace! What's going on?"

Not waiting for an invitation, he strode quickly into the room to stand beside the old four-poster. She was wearing a white cotton gown edged with tiny eyelet lace and was partially covered with a pink sheet. Her black hair was loose and fanned against the two pillows propping her head and shoulders. In spite of her tanned skin, she looked extremely pale. Fear for her and the baby rushed through him.

"Why are you here?" she asked curtly. "I thought you'd be gone by now."

"I'm packed, if that makes you any happier." He sat down on the edge of the bed and she shot him a glare of warning.

"What'll make me happy is to see the back of you."

Her eyes looked suspiciously red, as though it hadn't been too long ago since they'd been swimming with tears. He didn't like to think she'd been crying over him or for any reason.

"Not until you tell me what's wrong. Your violin students should have been here an hour ago."

Her gaze fell to the sheet. "How would you know?" she asked glumly.

"Because today is Tuesday. You told me you teach on Tuesday and Friday evenings."

The corners of her lips turned down in a mocking frown. "You actually remembered something like that, or were you taking notes on the suspect?"

"Don't be catty, Grace. It isn't you. Besides, you're too pretty to be that way."

Her gaze lifted back to his face and for a moment he could see pain flickering in the green depths. "Must you keep on lying? Or is that how it is with you lawyers, you do so much of it, you can't tell the difference?"

"I suppose I deserved that, otherwise I wouldn't be taking it, Grace. Not even from you. But if you really want to know, I hated lying to you. I wished I'd never started it."

"But you did," she said. Then with a weary sigh, she added, "I wish you'd just leave, Jack."

He folded his arms against his chest in a gesture that said he had no intention of going anywhere until she'd answered his questions.

"Is something wrong with the baby?"

She bit her lip, then twisted her head away from him. "No. Not yet," she whispered.

His hand come down on her shoulder and his fingers gripped her soft flesh. "What do you mean, not yet? Has something happened?"

She turned her head and met his gaze. "I—I'm having some problems and the doctor has ordered me to bed."

Something akin to panic shot through him, but there was no way he was going to let Grace see it. Even though he didn't know much about pregnancies, he understood Grace shouldn't be worried or upset.

"What sort of problems?"

"It's...too embarrassing to tell you."

"Now isn't the time for modesty, Grace. Anyway, I'm fully aware of the female anatomy. You're not going to embarrass me."

She took a deep breath, then let it out. Eventually the need to share her worrisome problem with someone outweighed her determination to rebuff him.

"This morning as I was going to class, I started leaking amniotic fluid. Do you understand what that is?"

He nodded. "It surrounds the baby in the womb. Like a cushion. So what does this mean? That you're going into labor?"

The concern in his voice sounded so real, she could almost believe he was actually worried about her. And maybe he was, she thought with sudden horror. Her baby was related to him. Maybe he'd changed his mind and was planning to try to get the child once it was born. The notion made her face turn a shade whiter.

"That's what the doctor doesn't want happening. He says the child will be much healthier if I can carry it for at least two more weeks. Especially his or her lungs. That's why he's ordered me off my feet. So the leak won't grow worse. Or, God forbid, a rupture won't occur."

"Why didn't he put you in the hospital?" Jack demanded. "This is crazy! You should be surrounded by nurses."

Grace shook her head. "I don't need nurses, Jack. Just rest. And the doctor is aware that I don't have medical insurance. He's trying to keep the expense minimal for me. Unless, of course, hospitalization is the only solution."

Jack scowled at her. "Money is not an issue here, Grace. If you need to be in the hospital, I'll—"

"I don't!" she swiftly cut in. "So forget it."

He eased the grip on her shoulder. "You can't take care of yourself like this. Who's going to see after you?"

She couldn't look at him. "I told the doctor I had someone here to help me."

"Sounds like you know how to do a bit of lying yourself," he said.

She glared at him. "But I will. As soon as I have a chance to make a few phone calls."

"To whom?"

"Just because I don't have family doesn't mean I don't have friends."

"I'm sure you do. But are any of them able to stay here with you for an indefinite period of time? Or are they tied up with jobs or classes?"

She swallowed hard and Jack knew he'd hit home. Except for him, Grace was totally alone.

"Probably," she muttered. "But there's always Miss Kate. I could go stay with her."

He couldn't prevent his fingers from meshing in the hair lying against her shoulders. As he rolled the silky texture between the pads of his thumb and forefinger he asked, "Who's Miss Kate?"

"My dearest friend, who lives just a minute or two away. She's eighty-five. But she's not decrepit. She'll help me."

He made a disgusted sound and she turned an insulted look on him.

"I told you I relate better to old people," she said.

"There's nothing wrong with that. But I'm afraid you're going to need more than Miss Kate for the next few days, Grace. You need me. And furthermore, you know it."

Her green eyes grew hard, her features tight. "You're the last person I need! I don't want you here."

Her words hurt even though he knew she had very good reason for saying them. "You want your baby to be born healthy, don't you?"

The rigid lines on her face eased and Jack felt the tenseness in her shoulder relax.

"More than anything."

"Then you'll have to put up with me. I don't see that you have any other choice."

Grace desperately wished there was some other choice. The last thing she wanted to do was to accept help from Jack. It grated her raw to think she had to be beholden to him in any way. It sickened her to think she and her baby would have to depend on a man who'd deliberately lied to her. But worse than the lies he'd told her, Jack had preyed upon her empty heart. He'd made her believe she was worthy, that she was more than just a poor shrimper's half-orphaned grandchild. He'd made her feel beautiful and wanted and that any worthwhile man would be proud and pleased to be in her company.

"I'm sure you have plenty of work waiting for you back in Houston," she said woodenly.

"I'd already promised you I would stay until the baby was born. This doesn't change anything about my work." Except that he realized how insignificant it seemed compared to the well-being of Grace and the baby.

"You said you were packed. You obviously want to go."

He grimaced. "You ordered me to go. Remember?"

She rolled toward him, her expression wary as she scanned his solemn face. "Why are you doing this,

Jack? You don't owe me anything. Are you doing this to ease your conscience?''

His fingers touched her cheek, then skimmed down the creamy line of her throat. And it dawned on him that touching Grace, under any circumstances, was a very precious privilege.

"My secretary would probably tell you I don't have a conscience and haven't had for years."

"I'm not surprised," she said, her voice rich with sarcasm. "Then what is your motive? Is this a scheme to try to gain rights to my baby?"

Her mistrust left him sick inside and he knew nothing he could say now would make her believe in him. He was going to have to prove his sincerity to her through deeds, not words.

"You're the baby's mother. He belongs with you. It appears Trent doesn't want the child. And I'll be the first one to say he doesn't deserve him. Why would *I* want to gain rights to your baby?"

She shrugged and her lashes fluttered down as confusion flickered in her eyes. "He or she has Barrett blood. Like you. Maybe you want your sister to have her grandchild to raise."

He shook his head. "Jillian will have other grandchildren. And though I love my sister, she's had her chance at raising her own son. And the results don't look too good to me." He placed his hand on Grace's stomach and felt a measure of comfort as he felt the baby move. "I happen to believe you deserve your own chance at raising your son. And I'm thinking you'll do a much better job."

If Grace thought she could believe just a portion of what he'd just said, she would forgive him. But his deceit had shaken the very foundation beneath her feet.

She could no longer trust her own judgment. She'd believed with her heart rather than her head. And she could never let herself be that gullible again.

Hardened with new resolve, she brushed his hand away and turned her back to him. "Pretty words, Jack. But then, you're good at that, aren't you? You've had years of experience. Years of drawing a person's focus off the real issue. I wouldn't believe you if you signed an affidavit."

He said nothing, and after a moment she felt his weight lift from the mattress, then heard the sound of his footsteps as he left the bedroom.

Moments later tears were streaming down her cheeks. Grace turned her face into the pillow and tried to sob away the ache in her heart.

Chapter Ten

"Where do you want me to sleep?"

Grace turned her head to see Jack was back beside her bed. His khaki trousers and cotton shirt had been changed to gray gym shorts and a faded black T-shirt. Nearly two hours had passed since he'd left her bedroom. During the past hour she'd heard him coming and going in the other rooms and she'd instinctively known he was moving his things into her house. Which was the only sensible thing to do under the circumstances, she supposed.

Yet his proposed question was enough to remind her how drastically her feelings had changed since she'd learned of his duplicity. Just yesterday it would have been a comfort to have his arms around her and to know he was no further than a whisper away. But tonight she could hardly bring herself to look at his handsome face.

"The guest bedroom will be fine," she said, her gaze purposely sliding away from the sight of him.

"I thought you might want me closer. In case you

needed me in the night. I could put a cot in here," he suggested.

Just having him in the house was killing her. To know he was sleeping only a few steps away would be unbearable.

"That isn't necessary," she said coolly.

He made a disgusted sound. "Grace, don't get the silly notion I'd try to take advantage of you."

Fresh anger burst like a tiny bomb inside her. "You've already done a good job of that, Jack."

His jaws tightened. "I meant in a sexual way, Grace."

Strange, Grace thought bitterly, but it felt as though Jack had taken advantage of her body, along with her head and her heart. There wasn't anything about her the man hadn't touched.

"Like I said, the guest room should be comfortable enough for the both of us."

"Fine," he snapped. "Are you allowed up for any reason?"

"Only for trips to the bathroom."

"Then I'll bring you something to eat in a few minutes. Is there anything else you need?"

A new heart, she wanted to say, *you crushed this one.* Out loud, she said, "No. I'm going to try to sleep."

Nodding, he turned away from the bed, but after two steps he paused and glanced back at her. "Grace, what are you going to do about your classes?"

She sighed. "There's nothing I can do."

"Will you have to take them over?"

That he even bothered to ask puzzled Grace. She could see why he might be concerned about the baby. But her music degree was something else. "Yes. I'll have missed too many class hours by the time I'm able to get up and go again."

"I'm sorry, Grace."

"Yes, I am, too." For so many things, she thought, but mostly for trusting you.

The next morning Grace woke to sounds in the kitchen and for one brief second, as the scent of bacon and coffee drifted to her nostrils, she imagined her grandfather was alive and cooking breakfast. As he placed the food on the table, he would call to her and afterward she would help him wash the dishes before she got ready for school.

But those innocent days were over and had been for a long, long time, Grace thought. It wasn't her grandfather in the kitchen now. It was Jack. And she didn't know how she was possibly going to survive the next two weeks with him so near.

"Time to eat," he announced.

She glanced around to see the object of her thoughts entering the bedroom with a breakfast tray.

He waited for her to scoot herself to a sitting position against the pillows, then carefully placed the tray across her thighs.

"This isn't cold cereal," she said as she glanced over the plate of food. Along with the bacon, scrambled eggs and toast, there was butter, jelly, juice and milk. He'd obviously gone to a great deal of trouble.

"I didn't want to give you cold cereal. It's bad enough that you can't get up without having to down a boring breakfast."

He pulled up a nearby wooden rocking chair and took a seat as though he planned to keep her company. It was on the tip of Grace's tongue to tell him she didn't need conversation with her food. But what he'd said last night was true. It just wasn't in her to be catty. He knew how she felt about him. She didn't have to keep sniping as a way to remind him.

"I didn't think you could cook."

He grinned. "Actually, I thought I wasn't all that bad of a cook, until this morning." He motioned toward the food on her tray. "That's the second attempt. The first one is in the garbage."

She took a bite of the bacon. "Surely it wasn't that bad."

He chuckled. "The bacon resembled strips of black tar paper and the toast wasn't far behind. The eggs could have posed for a piece of brown sponge. I've learned you can't hurry good food."

Grace glanced at him as she reached for the juice. "I don't expect you to cook for me, Jack. I can eat anything out of a can or the microwave. Did you fix yourself something?"

He nodded. "Some of the same. How are you feeling this morning?"

Grace could feel his eyes traveling over her and though she knew it was stupid, she was glad she'd brushed her hair and washed her face on her last trip to the bathroom.

"Weary from just laying in bed. Otherwise, I'm doing fine."

She went back to eating and for a while Jack was content to merely watch her. He'd spent most of last night worrying, imagining the worst, and wondering how he would feel or what he would do if something happened to Grace or the baby. Just the thought of losing either one of them struck him with horror, and that in itself worried him.

He'd only known Grace for about a week and in that length of time he'd done no more than kiss her. Yet she had done something to him.

He wasn't the same man who'd left Houston in an exhausted dither. For the first time in years, someone really meant something to him. But what good did that do, when she wanted no part of him? he wondered.

"I hope you won't mind, Grace, but I'm going to have to call my secretary and give her this phone number so it will be easier for her to relate back to me from the office. I'll try to keep the calls to a minimum and of course all the expense will be on me. As for my fax, I'll leave it connected in the bungalow. It won't be any trouble to walk over whenever I need it."

"The phone won't bother me," she said between bites of egg.

"I don't want you to feel like I'm invading your house or taking over."

Actually, Grace had felt invaded the moment she'd turned around and found him in her backyard. "You've been trying to take over ever since you've come to Biloxi. Why should now be any different?"

His brows lifted. "I haven't been trying to take over."

She made a little sound of disbelief. "First it was my music students, then the air conditioner, the money, the groceries. I'm sure I could think of more if I tried. But that's enough." She leveled a knowing look on him. "I believe you're a man who's used to having his own way. It's a good thing you don't want a wife. You'd make a lousy husband."

He leaned up in the rocker. "And you must be a hard woman to please. I just brought you breakfast in bed."

She smiled at him, but the expression didn't reach

her eyes. "And it's very nice. But one meal doesn't make up for your ills."

Jack was well aware she was talking about his concealment of the truth. Rising to his feet, he looked down at her. "Like you said, it's a good thing I don't want a wife. Take your time with breakfast. I'll be back for the tray."

Irene was stunned when, later that day, Jack called to tell her he'd be in Biloxi for at least two more weeks.

"Are you out of your mind, Jack? The pill case is scheduled on the court docket in less than three weeks! What if you're not here?"

"Marshall can handle it if I'm not back by then. In the meantime, I'm going to fax you all the notes I've written up so far. There's enough information in them to get him prepared."

He could hear Irene releasing a long breath. "Jack, I understand better than anyone that you needed time off. Especially away from this office. But this…isn't like you. Are you feeling okay? Have you checked your blood pressure since you've been down there?"

Jack's lips twisted. Taking his blood pressure would be useless. It rose every time he looked at Grace.

"I'm all right, Irene. Don't mother me."

"Mother you! I'd like to kick you in the—what are you doing down there anyway? Before you left you were going crazy over this pill case. Now it's like you don't give a damn."

He grimaced as he considered his secretary's words. He'd ruined the woman, he thought with sudden dawning. Over the years he'd pushed and badgered until Irene was consumed with the firm's success.

"Irene, look at the big picture. The only thing these

two companies are really fighting about is money. If the outcome of the trial would effect a patient's health, I would feel differently, but frankly, it means little to me which one wins."

Instead of the gasp of shock he'd expected, Irene was completely silent. After a while he was beginning to wonder if she'd laid down the phone and left the room.

"Irene? Damn it, can't you talk? Say something or I'm going to hang up."

"You're the one who'd better say something. Otherwise, I'm going to call 9-1-1 in Biloxi and have you carted off to the hospital. You've had a stroke or mental breakdown of some sort. Jack Barrett's main goal in life is to win."

Jack glanced toward the open door of Grace's bedroom. Since he was at the opposite end of the long living room, he very much doubted she could pick up his words. "My goals have changed, Irene. I've decided I need more of a reason than money to fight hard for a case. Now get your pen. I have a new phone number to give you. From now on you can reach me here."

He called out Grace's number to his secretary. After she'd repeated it back to him, she asked, "You've moved from the bungalow? Why? I thought you liked it?"

"I'm staying with someone next door."

Another long pause, then she said with knowing disgust, "A woman."

"What if it is?"

"You just swore off women forever," she reminded him. "Jack is she the reason—"

"It's not what you're thinking, Irene. She's young and pregnant and ill. She needs someone to look after her."

"Pregnant!" Irene practically shouted in his ear. "How could you look after her? You've never been around a pregnant woman in your life!"

"Well, I have now," he said angrily, then abruptly changed the subject. "Is Marshall in his office?"

"I think so."

"Tell him to call me at the number I gave you as soon as he has a free moment."

"All right. Is there anything else?" she asked brusquely.

"No. Just watch for the notes and see that Marshall gets them. I'll be sending more later."

"Jack?"

He let out a heavy breath. "Irene, if you start lecturing me again, I'm going to fire you. This instant."

"I was only going to ask you if Jillian has told you about Trent's engagement?"

"She called last night." Too bad he hadn't answered the phone before Grace had, he thought. A voluntary confession from him might have made her see the whole thing in a different light. As it was, she had him lumped with the scrubs.

Irene went on. "She came by the office this morning to give me the news. Your sister is on cloud nine. That boy is her whole life."

"Yeah," he said grimly. "I'm aware of that, Irene."

When Paul finally divorced Jillian, she should have gotten a life of her own. Instead, all these years she'd lived only for her son and in the process she'd spoiled him rotten. Jack had been stupid to think he could shield his sister from Trent's irresponsible behavior. The only reason Jillian was being spared a ton of heartache was Grace and the fact that she wasn't a greedy or vindictive woman.

"You don't sound too happy about the news," Irene said after a moment.

"On the contrary. I hope he's found a woman who'll give him everything he deserves," Jack told her, then quickly ended the conversation.

After a week of lying in bed Grace was going stir-crazy. She'd never been a person to just sit, much less lay, and it frustrated her greatly to not be able to walk outside and down to the beach or even to the kitchen for a drink of water.

But the leakage had stopped completely and the doctor was very satisfied with her progress. However, when she'd begged him to let her back onto her feet, he'd refused. He didn't want to take any chances and Grace hadn't argued with him. In the end it didn't matter what sort of misery she had to go through. She would do whatever necessary to make sure her baby was delivered healthy.

Throughout the past days, Jack had brought her stacks of books and magazines to read and had moved the television set into her bedroom for added entertainment. He'd hooked up a second telephone by the head of her bed and made sure she had everything she wanted to eat or drink. He'd kept her favorite nightgowns laundered and brought her a CD player with several CDs of classical violin music.

With Jack showing her so much kindness, she'd found it impossible to stay angry with him. And once her anger had vanished, so had the awful tension between them. It had been a relief for Grace to open up and talk with Jack again—about his work, the weather, their meals. They discussed anything other than his deception.

His company eased her confinement and she couldn't deny that he made her days much brighter. In spite of her initial resolve never to forgive him, her heart began to melt and soften. Yet she still couldn't totally believe he was doing it all just for her sake. She'd made that mistake once and she was determined not to do it again.

During the past week she'd had plenty of thinking time and she'd come to the conclusion that she'd actually been a lucky woman. If she hadn't discovered just who and what Jack was when she had, things between them might have gotten totally out of hand.

Looking back on it now, she could see that she'd been falling in love with him. But thank goodness that had all stopped once she'd learned of his deception. Even so, she still hurt whenever she looked at him, and the physical attraction she'd felt for him was just as deep and burning as ever. But the truth had opened Grace's eyes and she was looking at things from a realistic standpoint.

Jack's interest in her had been purely calculated. She didn't doubt that it still was. And even if he hadn't been lying about being Trent's uncle, he'd openly admitted he wasn't interested in marrying again. The most she would have ever gotten from Jack Barrett was a short affair. Which would have ruined any hope for Grace finding future happiness. Because, lies or not, she instinctively knew that having Jack as a lover would make all other men pale in comparison.

The sound of muffled voices in another part of the house caught her attention. She strained to catch more but it was impossible to tell if the voice belonged to a visitor or if Jack was back on the telephone. More than likely the latter. With each day that passed he seemed to spend more and more time with his work.

Grace told herself she was glad. The less she'd seen of him, the better off her silly, wounded heart would be. Yet she didn't like to think of him working so incessantly. When she saw the lines of fatigue on his face, she wanted to ease them away with her fingers. She wanted to tell him that nothing should matter so much.

A light tap on the doorjamb had her gaze swinging to the entrance of the bedroom. Jack was standing on the threshold, a faint smile on his handsome face.

"You have a visitor. I told her I wanted to make sure you were decent before she came in."

Grace instantly scooted up in the bed and smoothed the cover over her swollen stomach. Since she'd been confined to her bed, a few of her classmates had called to check on her. But no one had come to the house to actually see her. "A visitor? Who?"

He walked over to the bed. "A little gray-haired lady. She said her name was Kate."

"Miss Kate! How did she get here?" Grace exclaimed.

"Her son dropped her off on his way into town. Will she eat or drink anything if I offer it to her?"

The idea of Jack playing host just as if he were her husband touched Grace in a way she didn't want to think about.

"Miss Kate likes iced tea with lemon and sugar. Lots of lemon and sugar."

He made an okay signal with his thumb and forefinger. "Now what do you want?"

For things to be different, she thought. Oh, so, different. "Anything, Jack. I know you think I'm a hard woman to please. But I'm not. Really."

He moved a step closer and brought his forefinger gently beneath her chin. "I know you're not, Grace. If you were a hard woman to please, staying here would be a hell of a lot easier."

She frowned at him. "That doesn't make sense, Jack."

He patted her cheek, then as he headed toward the door he said, "Good. I don't want you to make sense of it."

Before Grace had time to think about his odd remark, Miss Kate walked through the door. She was wearing a calico dress, a straw sun hat and tennis shoes.

The sight of her dear, wrinkled face brought tears to Grace's eyes and she held out her hand to the older woman.

"Miss Kate, you didn't have to go to all the trouble of coming to see me."

Kate's bony fingers squeezed Grace's hand. "And what if I wanted to?"

Grace smiled. "Then I'm very glad you did."

Kate patted Grace's shoulder. "How are you, child?"

"I'm doing good. But the doctor still won't let me up. He says five more days and then I can get back on my feet. By then it should be safe for me to deliver."

"And he expects that to happen once you get up and get to moving around?"

Smiling wanly, Grace answered, "Yes. I can hardly wait. I'm so tired of this bed. And I'm ready to see my baby."

Kate nodded as she swept the sun hat off the gray braid wrapped around the top of her head. "I'm ready, too."

"I'm sorry I haven't been able to do your laundry, Miss Kate. But as soon as I can take the baby out, I'll be over to help you."

The old woman chuckled and waved her hand

through the air. "I don't give a dang about the laundry. It's your fiddlin' I miss. And your company."

Grace's expression turned suddenly wistful. "I'll bet none of your children ever got themselves into this much of a mess. I'm almost glad Granddaddy isn't here to see me. He'd be ashamed."

Kate shook her finger at Grace. "He wouldn't be any such thing. Your grandpa wasn't perfect. None of us are."

"No," Grace glumly agreed. "But I wanted him to be proud of me. Especially after the way mother turned out. I hate to think I'm headed down the same road as her."

Kate opened her mouth to say something but at the same moment Jack walked through the door carrying a tray of refreshments.

Grace watched the old woman as she openly eyed Jack from head to toe.

"Grace thought you might like some iced tea, Miss Kate," he said to her as he handed her the cold glass.

While Jack handed a second glass to Grace, Kate took a cautious sip.

"Pretty good," she admitted. "Not as smooth as Grace's, but close."

The compliment brought a chuckle from Jack and Grace thought how strange it must feel for him to be doing something as mundane as serving someone a glass of tea. From the bits and pieces she'd gleaned about his life, she knew he was a man who spent most of his time in the courtroom and his money on employees to do his bidding. Now he was doing it for others.

"Thank you, Miss Kate. I appreciate that."

"What do you do, young man?"

He stood at the foot of Grace's bed. "I'm a lawyer. I have a law firm in Houston, Texas."

"I was in Houston once. Back in the fifties. Too big for me. But Texas is a pretty place. I like the bluebonnets." She continued to study him with a keen eye. "A lawyer you say. Hmm. That's something. Are you a good one?"

The corners of Jack's lips curled upward with fond appreciation. Anyone who cared about Grace stood well with him. "I like to think so. Why? Do you have a legal problem you need help with?"

"No. But I might sometime...when I get old. A person never knows what the future holds."

"Jack is the man who was staying in the bungalow next door, Miss Kate." Grace felt the need to explain.

The old woman glanced at Grace. "I remember you tellin' me about him," she said, then to Jack, she asked, "How long you plannin' on stayin'?"

His gaze settled on Grace. "Until Grace has the baby. Then I'll be heading back to Houston."

Just hearing him say he'd be leaving soon tore at Grace's heart. Although she didn't know why. She didn't want him hanging around forever. She had to get on with her life and he with his. She needed to forget the pleasure and the pain he'd given her.

"That's too bad. Grace is gonna need some help after the baby gets here."

"Miss Kate!" Grace said with a gasp. "This isn't the old days. As soon as I have the baby I'll be back on my feet in two or three days. I can take care of myself. And anyway, Jack has important work waiting on him. He can't stay here."

The old woman scowled at her. "I never said he could stay. I just said it was too bad he couldn't."

Grace sighed and Jack realized it was time for him to make a quick exit.

"I'm going back to work," he said. "Call me if you need me."

Kate watched him disappear out the door, then she leaned up in the rocker to bring herself closer to Grace. "Honey, you can't let him go. He's a real live one."

Grace supposed in Kate's terms "a live one" translated to hunk. She frowned at the old woman. "Looks aren't everything, Miss Kate. Why, I've heard you say from time to time that Walter wasn't anything to look at, but he was a wonderful husband to you."

The old woman made an exasperated gesture with her hand. "I'm not talking about looks, child. Although, I have to admit your Jack is more than enough to make a woman lose her head."

Didn't she know it, Grace thought grimly. "Then what are you talking about? His money?"

Kate's expression turned to one of disappointment. "I ain't ever had much money. Don't care if I ever do," she snapped.

"Then what—"

"I'm talking about love," Kate cut in. "He's got it for you, honey. He just don't know it yet."

Grace's mouth fell open, then she burst out with a caustic laugh. "Oh, no, Miss Kate! You don't understand. Jack isn't helping me because—" She broke off with a bitter grimace, than passing a hand over her face, she tried again. "Jack is Trent's uncle. He didn't tell me at first. I found out on my own a few days ago. I was so angry I told him to leave. But—he wouldn't go after he found out I was having health problems."

Kate's thin white brows lifted suggestively. "Wonder why that was?" she mused out loud.

Grace's features grew tight as she unnecessarily adjusted the sheet and blanket covering her stomach. "That's something I haven't figured out yet. But I think—well, the only thing I can figure is he wants to try to take the baby from me. He probably doesn't believe I can give it the financial security he thinks it should have."

"Bah!"

Grace turned a pointed look on her. "Don't you understand what I've been saying? Jack lied to me. He purposely misled me. And I trusted him!"

"Did he have a reason for not telling you he was that rascal's uncle?"

Grace plucked at the cover as she quickly related Jack's whole version of the story to Kate. Ending with, "He says he was just trying to protect his family. Because he didn't know me."

Kate tapped a finger thoughtfully against the rocker arm. "It must have been a big shock to him. Comin' down here and findin' you pregnant with his nephew's child."

"If you ask me, they're two birds of the same feather," Grace said bitterly. "The uncle is no better than the nephew."

"How do you figure that?"

Grace's brows lifted with mocking disbelief. "Do you have to ask? They both lied to me. They both deceived me for their own gain."

Kate shook her head. "No, child. Your Jack wasn't lying for himself. He was trying to protect his sister. There's a big difference between the two men. And you're missing the biggest one of all."

Grace shot her a puzzled look. "And what's that?"

"Trent ran off and deserted you. Jack is still here. If that doesn't tell you something, then you'd better get some glasses for those pretty peepers of yours."

Chapter Eleven

The next evening Miss Kate's words were still lingering in Grace's thoughts, troubling her far more than being a prisoner to the bed.

She couldn't argue that Jack had been wonderful to her these past days. In fact, she'd seen sides of him that had completely surprised her. The hard, cynical, and very impatient man she'd first met seemed to be gone. This new Jack was gentle and kind, even sweet. And he did more than fetch and carry for her, he took time out from his work to sit and talk with her, to bolster her spirits, to encourage her to think of the near future when she would be out of bed and caring for her new son.

A wry smile touched Grace's lips. This past week, Jack continued to predict the baby would be a boy. He wouldn't consider there was a fifty-fifty chance that the child could be either sex. It was almost as if he *wanted* the baby to be a boy. She sometimes even got the strange impression he was looking forward to its coming as though *he* was its father.

Frowning with self-disgust, Grace scooted up in the bed and reached for the hairbrush lying on the nightstand. As she scraped the bristles against her scalp, she told herself she'd been lying in bed so long she was beginning to imagine things.

Maybe Jack had been extra kind and considerate to her. And maybe he had shown concern and interest for the baby. But that didn't mean he loved her or wanted her in his life.

The brush suddenly paused halfway down the length of her long black hair. Did she want Jack to love her? Did she want to be his wife?

With a groan of anguish she dropped the brush in her lap, then covered her face with both hands. Since the moment she'd learned he'd lied to her, she'd been telling herself she hated him. She'd been trying her best to convince herself that she was only tolerating his presence because there was no one else to help her. Yet deep down, when she thought of the day he would be leaving, a black emptiness filled her heart. She couldn't imagine the days and coming months ahead without seeing his face, the frowns and smiles, the crinkles at the corners of his pale gray eyes, or not being able to hear his deep timbered voice.

She might as well face it, Grace thought miserably. She'd fallen in love with the man. The moment he'd strode into her backyard, he'd also walked straight into her heart. Even lying to her hadn't been enough to put a stop to her wayward feelings.

So what was she going to do now? Her baby would be coming in a week or so. She was desperate to finally have her child with her. Yet its arrival would mean losing Jack. How could so much joy be coupled with so much pain? she wondered. Moreover, how was she going to survive it?

The tormenting question was suddenly pushed aside as she caught the sound of the front door being opened, followed by a series of thumps and thuds on the floor. Earlier Jack had told her he was going to town to run a few errands, he must have returned with another trunkload of grocery sacks.

"Jack, is that you?"

"Yeah, but I'm busy. I'll be there in a minute or two."

She thought she heard another male voice and then the door opened and closed at least two more times. Eventually, his head appeared around the open door and her heart winced at the broad grin on his face.

"How are you feeling?"

In the past few days the question had become an hourly thing with him. And though Grace wished he was asking out of love, in reality she knew it was simply concern for his great nephew.

"I'm fine," she said. At least, her body was doing fine. She just couldn't say the same for her heart.

"Good. Because I have something to show you."

She looked at him skeptically. "You've bought too many groceries to fit in the refrigerator?"

He chuckled. "No. I haven't even been to the grocery store. But I have been shopping." He stepped into the bedroom and came to stand beside her. "Do you think it would hurt if I carried you out to the living room?"

"Did I hear another voice in there?" she asked suspiciously.

"A delivery boy. But he's gone now."

She pulled on a thin cotton robe, then scooted to the

edge of the bed. "If it's that important, then I'll just walk to the bedroom door and look into the living room," she told him. "I'm far too heavy for you to carry."

"No! You're not supposed to walk any further than the bathroom," he argued as he bent to pick her up. "I'm not a weakling. I carried you for a much further distance on the beach, remember?"

"I remember," she murmured huskily as she curled her arms around his neck.

He lifted her up and against his chest, then looked into her face, which was only inches away. From the moment he'd held this woman in his arms, he'd wanted her. But not until these past days, with the baby's health threatened, had he really come to realize the extent of his feelings for Grace. He didn't just want her anymore, he loved her. He didn't just need to know her future and the baby's would be financially secure; he wanted to be the one to make it that way. He needed them to make his life complete—to make it mean something worthwhile. Yet he wasn't the least bit sure she would believe what was in his heart.

"I haven't forgotten anything about that day, Grace," he said. "I still want you just as much as I did then."

His admission tore a hole right through her. She closed her eyes as a tiny moan sounded in her throat. "Jack, don't—"

"Grace, I know you can't forgive me for not telling you who I was. But I'm asking you to try. The baby will be coming soon. And I—can't go back to Houston thinking you still hate me."

She turned her face into his shoulder and struggled to keep her tears hidden deep inside her. "You'd better take me into the living room. We can't—talk about anything standing here like this," she said, her voice muffled by his shirt.

"All right," he agreed. "Close your eyes until I tell you to open them."

"Why?"

"Don't ask why, just do as I say," he ordered gently.

Grace closed her eyes, then felt the strength of his body as he carried her out of the bedroom. Moments later the cushions of the couch were against her back and she was forced to release her hold around his neck.

Squatting on his heels beside her, he said, "Okay, you can look now."

Instinctively Grace's eyes focused first on Jack's face. There was a smug little smile on his face and he made a sideways motion with his head, urging her to look to her left. When she did, her eyes grew wide and her lips parted with astonishment.

A whole group of baby furniture made of dark polished wood was clustered together on the living room floor.

"Oh! Oh, my!"

She began to push herself up from the cushions, but before she could sit all the way up, Jack gently pushed her back down.

"No. You stay where you are. I'll bring everything closer so you can have a better look," he told her.

"Jack! It's beautiful! Where—did all this come from?"

With a sheepish grin, he carried the cradle over to the couch and placed it on the floor so that it would be close enough for her to touch.

"It took me a little while to find a baby boutique, but I finally managed. I've been doing a little shopping," he answered her question.

"A little shopping! The baby will be ten years old before it needs anything else!" she exclaimed.

Along with the cradle, there was a big crib and mattress, a large chest, plus a dressing table. From where she lay on the couch, she could see the crib was piled high with packages of baby clothes, diapers, bedding and stuffed toys.

"It's all made of cherry wood," he told her as he watched her run her fingers over the edge of the cradle. "And when he gets big enough for a twin bed, they have one to match everything. Do you like it?"

Her head swung back and forth in amazement. "It's—I don't know what to say," she said in a choked voice. "I—I can't imagine having anything so beautiful for the baby. But you—"

He eased down onto the couch on a empty space next to her legs. "You told me you were going to fix a nursery in the empty bedroom next to yours. It wouldn't be much of a nursery without furniture."

Jack pushed the cradle into a rock and she couldn't stop the smile from curving her lips as she imagined the baby lulled to sleep by the gentle motion.

"I cleaned the room out some time ago with hopes of making it into a nursery someday. When I had enough saved up to buy a bit of secondhand furniture. But this—" Her gaze lifted to his face. "It's real cherry wood! It must have cost a fortune! You shouldn't have done this, Jack."

He reached for her hand and was thrilled when she didn't pull away from him. "Grace, for the first time I can ever remember, I enjoyed buying something. I've had money all my life, but it never really meant anything to me. And now I know why. I didn't have anyone to share it with."

She looked at him with disbelief. "You had your wife at one time."

His lips twisted with sarcasm as he shook his head. "No. Lenore didn't want to *share* anything. She expected and demanded all that I could give her and more." His features softened as his eyes scanned her face. "But I think—when I give to you—I believe it really means something to you. Am I wrong?"

Tears suddenly blurred her vision and before he could stop her, she raised up and flung her arms around his neck. "Oh, Jack, everything you've done for me means something. Don't you know that by now?" she whispered against his cheek.

His hands came against her back where his fingers meshed in her long, silky hair. "Does this mean you've forgiven me?"

She leaned her head back far enough to look into his eyes. "You didn't buy all this just to make amends, did you?"

"No. It's for you and the baby because you needed it and I wanted you to have it. That's the only reason."

She swallowed hard as her fingers touched the hard line of his jaw. "You—you're not planning on trying to take the baby from me. I thought at first you were. But now—"

"Grace!" he said with an accusing groan. "How could you think that?"

Her head swung ever so slightly back and forth. "Don't you understand, Jack? Other than Granddaddy, no one has ever cared enough to do anything for me. That's why it's been hard for me to believe you're not doing all this for other reasons."

"Well, believe it," he said flatly. Then with a rueful grimace, he went on. "But I guess you still regard everything that comes out of my mouth a lie. And if you do—I can't blame you. But you and the baby are important to me, Grace. More important than you'll ever know.''

She closed her eyes and took a deep breath. Touching him again, smelling the scent of his hair and skin, feeling the warmth of his body next to hers was the most wonderful thing she'd ever experienced. He'd become a part of her. Without him, she would wither.

''Oh, Jack, I've forgiven you for all that days ago,'' she murmured.

One hand came around to gently cup her chin and she opened her eyes to see the doubt on his face.

''You sure could have fooled me,'' he said. ''I haven't seen a smile on your face since—well, since our picnic.''

A pain pierced her heart as she wished for that magic time again. Yet she realized it would never be. Jack had another life in Houston. He would be gone soon. And even if she could talk him into staying a bit longer, eventually it wouldn't work. He was not a man to stay idle. He had to work, to be in the courtroom for some reason or another. And, anyway, the baby would be here. Trent's baby. It would be expecting too much to ask him to forget it was his nephew's child and treat it as his own.

''I haven't been smiling because I—'' She broke off as what she really wanted to say warred with the sensible part of her. Because I love you, Jack. And I don't want you to go. I want us to be together. As a family, for always.

''Because why?'' he urged.

''I've been worried.'' She blurted the first thing she could think of.

"Worried! Damn, Grace, that's—"

This time it was Jack who suddenly stopped in mid-sentence. But this time the interruption was a knock on the door that had both their heads swiveling toward the sound.

"Who could that be?" Jack asked as he eased away from her.

Grace was just as puzzled. She rarely ever had callers unless it was her violin students or the rare occasion when Miss Kate came by. "Maybe the delivery boy forgot something? Or it could be one of my students."

Rising from the couch, Jack glanced at the furniture and baby accessories. "I don't think it's the delivery boy again. I'll go see."

While he went to answer the door, Grace relaxed back against the throw pillows piled into one corner of the couch.

She was reaching for a little brown teddy bear propped in one corner of the cradle when she heard Jack ask, "What are you doing here?"

It wasn't so much the question as the hard, demanding tone of his voice that caused her to turn her head around to where he stood at the open door.

"Jack? Who is it?" she asked him.

Grim-faced, Jack glanced at her, then for an answer, he pushed the door wider and the caller stepped inside. Even though she was half sitting, half lying on the couch, Grace still thought she might faint as Trent turned toward her.

"Hello, Grace."

She stared in stunned silence as he slowly walked toward her. His appearance hadn't changed. He was tall and lanky, his short blond hair combed into a neat, preppy style. His expensive, casual trousers and loafers were the same style he'd worn when he was here before. As was the gold watch on his wrist. Everything about him was the same as she remembered from months ago. Yet he looked so different and it dawned on her that she was seeing him through totally different eyes this time. And compared to Jack, he was just a shallow, rich boy, who didn't know the first thing about really loving or caring for a woman.

"What are you doing here?" she reiterated Jack's question.

"I—" He glanced around as Jack shut the door, then came to stand a few steps away from him. "What are you doing here, Uncle Jack?"

His face as smooth as granite, Jack nodded toward Grace. "I think you should answer the lady's question first, don't you?"

A crimson color suddenly appeared on Trent's cheeks and Grace figured Jack's strong presence was more than enough to bring Trent down from his pedestal.

"I wanted to talk to you, Grace," he said bluntly.

Her brows lifted with skepticism. "Haven't you heard of a telephone?"

Shrugging, he jammed his hands into his pockets, then cast another unsettled glance at his uncle.

"I wanted to do this in person. I figured I owed you that much. Since I—well, since I haven't seen you in a while."

"You mean since you got her pregnant then ran out on her?" Jack asked, his voice quiet yet clearly menacing.

Trent turned a look of surprise on his uncle. "What do you know about this?"

"Enough," he snapped.

Frowning, Trent shifted his weight from one foot to

the other. "Uncle Jack, would you mind terribly if Grace and I talked alone? This is between the two of us."

Jack cast a questioning look at Grace and her heart melted.

"Do you want me to go?" he asked her.

For the past week Grace had known she needed Jack. But not until this very moment did she realize how much she needed his strength, his kindness, and most of all his love. If she wasn't sure he would scold her for getting on her feet, she would've left the couch to go to him.

Instead she gently shook her head at Jack, then to Trent she said, "Whatever you have to say to me, Jack hears, too."

Trent's gaze slipped from her to Jack then back again. "So it's that way with you two."

As if Jack could read Grace's mind, he went to the couch and eased down beside her. His hand rested possessively on the calf of her leg.

"Get on with what you came to say, Trent," Jack told him.

Trent took a deep breath, then let it out, and Grace had to secretly smile. Knowing Trent, he'd not been a bit nervous or bothered about coming here to face her. Even after leaving her in the lurch the way he had. But facing Jack was obviously unnerving him in a big way.

"Well, I—I've recently become engaged," he said.

"Your mother has already sent us the word," Jack informed him. "We know."

Trent's nervous expression turned to something close to panic. "She—uh, you didn't say anything about Grace to her, did you?"

"Only because I didn't want Grace to be hurt. By either one of you."

Trent visibly relaxed. "Oh. That's good. You know Mom wouldn't understand about all this."

"No," Jack said dryly. "That's because she doesn't really know you."

Trent frowned. "Well, she wouldn't hate me. She's not *that* narrow-minded."

"No. Now that I think about it, she's pretty much let you have your way all these years. But this time you're probably worried she might cut the money off or tell this new fiancée of yours."

His features grew tight. "You're not being fair, Uncle Jack. From what I've seen, you don't exactly live the perfect model of moral righteousness."

"I've never professed to being anything close to perfect," he admitted. "And if I do let my morals slip, I make damn sure it's not going to hurt anyone but me. But you—you didn't care how much your lies or self-indulgence hurt Grace. You were only thinking about yourself. And if my guess is right, you're here now because you're still thinking about yourself."

"I want to make sure Grace isn't going to show up at my wedding, for Pete's sake!"

Grace let out a short, caustic laugh. "What conceit! I could care less who or when you marry."

"Maybe you don't," he said to her curtly, "but you might show up to demand child support."

Knowing how Trent's words must be hurting her, Jack reached for Grace's hand and squeezed it with gentle reassurance.

"The only thing I ever wanted you to give this child was a little bit of acknowledgment from you," she said to Trent. "Just so that he or she would know its father.

But I can safely say I don't even want that now. I don't ever want this child to be exposed to such a sorry example."

Trent looked at her angrily. "You're in no position to act haughty with me. You don't have a dime. I can afford to give you child support if that's what you're wanting."

"Didn't you hear her? She doesn't," Jack said sharply.

"Look, Uncle Jack, that's why I came down here. I know Grace doesn't have any money and I want to get this resolved before my wedding. I don't want Mother or my fiancée to know about Grace or the baby. It would only cause unnecessary problems."

"Grace is the one I don't want having any unnecessary problems," Jack countered.

Trent frowned at his uncle. "I understand Grace will need financial help for the baby. I'm willing to—"

"You don't understand anything," Jack cut in. "You left the most wonderful woman you could have ever possibly found. You could've had a child, a beautiful family, but you threw it all away. You weren't man enough to even see what you had."

Trent was suddenly looking at the baby furniture and the sight of his uncle sitting next to Grace, her hand clutched in his. "Looks like my loss is your gain."

Grace looked at Jack and what she saw in his eyes made her heart leap with hope and wonder. Could he really want her and the baby? Before she had time to think about it, Jack was saying, "Once I met Grace and got to know her, there was never any danger of this baby or Grace not being taken care of, Trent. I'd already planned to take up the responsibility and it's a job I'm happy to accept. Do you think you can live with that?

Will it bother you to know I'm raising your son as my own?''

Trent looked at the two of them, then smiled wryly. "As far as I'm concerned the baby is and always will be yours, Uncle Jack. I think I've got a lot of living and learning to do before I could ever be a father. At least, before I could be a good one. And I hope neither one of you will hate me for relinquishing all my rights.''

"I can't hate you, Trent. Not when I've gained so much," Jack told him. "But I can't speak for Grace. She's the one you wronged.''

Grace shook her head as she wound her arm through Jack's and pressed herself close to his side. "I never hated you, Trent. And even if I had, I couldn't now. This whole thing brought Jack and me together. Maybe you and your new wife will be as happy as the two of us. I sincerely hope you are.''

He nodded and his smile was humble as he said, "Well, it looks like there's not anything else I can say, except thanks to you both. And good luck. I'll be heading back to Houston tonight.''

Jack rose from the couch and walked his nephew to the door.

"Will you and Grace be moving to Houston soon?'' Trent asked as he stepped onto the porch.

Jack smiled as a feeling of excitement began to pour through him. Now that he knew where things stood with Trent, there was nothing left standing in the way of him making a new life with Grace and the baby.

"No. I don't think Houston's the place for us.''

Trent was clearly surprised by his answer. "What about the firm?''

"It will have to go on without me.''

* * *

After Trent drove away, Jack closed the door and returned to Grace, who was still on the couch.

She looked at him anxiously at he sat down beside her.

"Jack, I know I took a few liberties a moment ago with Trent by giving him the impression the two of us were—well, that we were going to be living together. But I could see—"

"That I love you?"

The breath whooshed out of her. "When did you decide that?"

His smile was full of puzzlement and joy. "I'm not sure. Maybe it was when I saw you standing over Joshua, telling him he would soon be playing Strauss or maybe it was when you served me iced tea after I had behaved like a jackass. I don't know. Since that day we picnicked and swam in the ocean, I knew I couldn't leave here and never see you again. Even if you did think I was the biggest liar you'd ever met."

She shook her head as she reached for his hands. "Oh, Jack, I've been telling myself I'd been a fool to let myself fall in love with you. Your life is—"

"Is going to change. Thanks to you."

"We're so different," she said, her voice full of doubt. "I could never fit into your life-style. I'm not so sure I'd want to if I could. I want to bring the baby up in a quiet, family home."

"Like this one?"

She nodded and he reached out and ran his hand lovingly over the side of her wavy black hair.

"And I understand your work, your life, is in Houston," she went on. "I couldn't ask you to leave it."

He groaned at the sight of her troubled expression.

"Grace, I heard you just tell Trent we were going to be very happy together."

"That was my wishful thinking speaking out loud."

"Oh, darling," he said as he pulled her into the circle of his arms. "We *are* going to be happy. Very happy."

"You said you never wanted to marry again. You said you were as happy as a hog in a watermelon patch being single."

"Why do you have to remember something like that? That was before I knew what it was like to really love someone," he murmured as his nose nuzzled the soft spot beneath her ear. "That was before you made me see there's a whole other world out there and I was missing it."

"But your work—"

"Has been killing me. It took a doctor's orders to get me out of the office. But you're what really made me see how I truly felt about my work."

She leaned her head back to study his face. "And how do you feel about it?" she asked.

"Not good. And I haven't in a long, long time. Maybe I never did," he seriously admitted. "I became a lawyer to please my father and I believed in doing so, it would also please me. But I realize now that I need more, Grace. I want to do something worthwhile, something other than transferring one huge settlement of money from one company to another."

She said, "I've never had the privilege of seeing you in the courtroom, but I'm positive you're very good at what you do. It would be a shame to waste your talent. But if it's making you unhappy, I'd be the first one to urge you to give it up."

His smile was full of wonder as his fingers touched

her cheek. "You're years younger than me, yet you see things so wisely."

She shook her head. "No. Not all things, Jack. I didn't see the true side of Trent before it was too late. But I can't regret the baby." Her eyes softly searched his. "Did you really mean it when you told Trent you intended to raise the child as your own?"

His hands slipped to her stomach and he grinned as the baby moved against his palms. "He *is* mine. I staked claims on him and you a long time ago. You just didn't realize it."

She laughed as joy and love poured into her heart, instantly healing the aching hole she'd had before Jack had come into her life.

"I think it took you a while to realize it, too," she teased, then her expression grew serious. "But if you want to move back to Houston, we will. You'll just have to give me a few days to recover after I have the baby."

Jack quickly shook his head. "I just told Trent a few moments ago that we're not going to Houston. I think right here, where we are is pretty fine. I've been studying about what I want to do about a job and I've decided I want to be a victim's advocate. Helping you and the baby has changed me, Grace. And I know helping others will be good, too. Biloxi is large enough for one more practicing lawyer. It won't be a problem to find a small office building. And as for you and your music, I have another idea."

Her smile was full of amazement. "You've been thinking about that, too?"

He chuckled as his hands slid upward to cup her full breasts. "Among other things," he admitted. "But you've already agreed that you really don't want to move away from here to teach music. And since money is not an issue, I'd like to build a music center of sorts, where any child, rich or poor can come to learn to play Strauss or Chopin.''

Grace's laughter bubbled out like the sweet music she would someday teach. ''The music won't be restricted to Strauss or Chopin. I'm even going to teach the style and tunes of Bob Wills and the Texas Playboys. After all,'' she added slyly, ''I'm marrying a Texas playboy. It would be appropriate, don't you think?''

He groaned and pulled her tightly against him. ''My playing days have just started. With you.''

She pressed her cheek against the precious thud of his heart. ''Does that mean you're going to sleep with me tonight?'' she asked hopefully.

''Sleep, yes. The rest will have to wait a few weeks.''

He lifted her head away from his chest and kissed her for long, sweet moments.

''I'm sorry about that, Jack,'' she whispered with longing and regret.

The sound of love and contentment purred deep in his throat. ''Don't be, my darling Grace. A few more weeks isn't going to kill me. But right now I'm going to get you back to bed. You've been sitting up too long and it's time I made us something for supper.''

She didn't object, but once he'd carried her back to the bedroom and placed her gently on the bed, she caught his hand and pulled him down next to her.

He looked at her with a quizzical smile on his face.

''There's one more thing I want to tell you, Jack,'' she said.

''That you love me?''

Smiling, she trailed her fingers along the strong line of his jaw. ''Along with the fact that I love you,'' she said. "I wanted to point out to you that I didn't ask if a victim's advocate made much money, because I don't care if you only make a modest salary. In fact, I don't care if you've been lying all this time and you don't have a dime to your name."

He chuckled. "The baby boutique might not like it if my checked bounced. It was rather a hefty one."

She shook her head as she tried to keep from smiling. "I'm serious, Jack. If you want to give away all your money. Or if you want me to sign a prenuptial agreement saying I won't inherit any of it, I'll be more than glad to. Because I don't ever want you to have any doubts about my love for you."

His expression suddenly grave, he leaned closer to nuzzle his cheek against hers. "I don't have any doubts," he promised.

"But I'm in a needy position right now. And when you look back on this time you might get to thinking I took the easy way out by marrying you."

His laughter mocked her argument. "This from a woman who forced me to take her last ten dollars for working on her air conditioner? I know you, Grace. You're a giver. Not a taker. You always will be." He lifted his head to look at her. "And there won't be any damn prenuptial agreement. This thing with us is going to be for a lifetime. And I want whatever's mine to be yours, too. Understand?"

She nodded meekly. "Yes," she murmured, "but do you understand I have nothing to give you in return but my love?"

A slow tender smile spread across his face. "That's all I'll ever ask from you, sweet Grace. But you might consider giving me another child or two, to go with this one, if you'd like."

For an answer she pulled his head down and whispered against his lips. "I'll work on that just as soon
as I can. But right now it would be very nice if you
would kiss me."

She felt his lips curve into another smile. "It's past
time to eat. Aren't you hungry?"

"For you, Jack."

He stretched out beside her and for a long, long
while, supper was forgotten.

Five days later Grace and Jack were married. Three
days after that, Jack Elias Barrett was born. He weighed
nearly eight pounds and his hair was as black as his
mother's. His father insisted little Jack's baby-blue eyes
would soon turn as green Grace's, too. And she wasn't
about to argue with her husband's prediction. After all,
he'd been right about the baby's sex. And he'd been
right about another very important thing. They were
happy together. Happy as hogs in a watermelon patch.

*   *   *   *   *

✒ *Silhouette* ROMANCE™

He's experienced and sophisticated.
He's mature, complex...and a little jaded.
But most of all, he's every woman's dream.

He's

◖ AN OLDER MAN

Don't miss this exciting new promotion from
Silhouette Romance and your favorite authors!

In June 2000 look for
PROFESSOR AND THE NANNY
by Phyllis Halldorson, Silhouette Romance #1452
Nanny Brittany Baldwin was the answer to single dad
Ethan Thorpe's prayers. But that was before the lovely
young caretaker started showing up in his dreams....

In July 2000 Stella Bagwell brings you
FALLING FOR GRACE
Silhouette Romance #1456
One glance at his alluring new neighbor had
Jack Barrett coming back for more. But the cynical
lawyer knew Grace Holliday was too young and
innocent—even if she was pregnant....

Only from

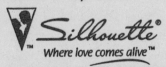

✒ *Silhouette*®

Where love comes alive™

Available at your favorite retail outlet.

COMING NEXT MONTH

#1462 THOSE MATCHMAKING BABIES—Marie Ferrarella
Storkville, USA
With the opening of her new day-care center, Hannah Brady was
swamped. Then twin babies appeared at the back door! Luckily
Dr. Jackson Caldwell was *very* willing to help. In fact, Hannah
soon wondered if his interest wasn't more than neighborly....

#1463 CHERISH THE BOSS—Judy Christenberry
The Circle K Sisters
Abby Kennedy was not what Logan Crawford had expected in his
new boss. The Circle K's feisty owner was young, intelligent...and
beautiful. And though Abby knew a lot about ranching, Logan was
hoping *he* could teach *her* a few things—about love!

#1464 FIRST TIME, FOREVER—Cara Colter
Virgin Brides
She was caring for her orphaned nephew. He had a farm to run and a
toddler to raise. So Kathleen Miles and Evan Atkins decided on a
practical, mutually beneficial union...until the handsome groom
decided to claim his virgin bride....

#1465 THE PRINCE'S BRIDE-TO-BE—Valerie Parv
The Carramer Crown
As a favor to her twin sister, Caroline Temple agreed to pose as
handsome Prince Michel de Marigny's betrothed. But soon she
wanted to be the prince's real-life bride. Yet if he knew the truth,
would Michel accept *Caroline* as his wife?

#1466 IN WANT OF A WIFE—Arlene James
Millionaire Channing Hawkins didn't want romance, but he
needed a mommy for his daughter. Lovely Jolie Winters was a
perfect maternal fit, but Channing soon realized he'd gotten more
than he'd wished for...and that love might be part of the
package....

#1467 HIS, HERS...OURS?—Natalie Patrick
Her boss was getting married, and perfectionist Shelley Harriman
wanted everything flawless. But Wayne Perry, her boss's friend,
had entirely different ideas. Could these two get through planning
the wedding...and admit there might be another in *their* future?

CMN0700